MAN OF
Her Dreams

Lorie O' Clare
Elizabeth Lapthorne

ELLORA'S CAVE
ROMANTICA PUBLISHING

What the critics are saying...

ℰ

In Her Dreams

"Ms. O'Clare has added to her Lunewulf series with a very good book. Samantha and Johann heat up the pages with their love and attraction. A fun, sexy book filled with hot sex and werewolves." ~ *The Romance Studio*

"In Her Dreams is hot, sexy and thoroughly enjoyable. Even if you're not familiar with the two previous Lunewulf installments, this is a great story, full of personality and witty dialogue." ~ *Romantic Times Reviews*

"A wonderfully romantic story. [...] The characters are very likeable and the sex scenes very hot. Lunewulf 3: In Her Dreams is a touching romantic story and one that should not be missed." ~ *In The Library Reviews*

Hide and Seek

"The sex scenes are hot [...] I quite enjoyed the book, and will definitely read it again." ~ *Fallen Angel Reviews*

"Hide and Seek is a great old fashioned story [...] A great story, that is defiantly worth the time to read." ~ *Just Erotic Romance Reviews*

An Ellora's Cave Romantica Publication

www.ellorascave.com

Man of Her Dreams

ISBN 141995086X, 9781419950865
ALL RIGHTS RESERVED.
In Her Dreams Copyright © 2004 Lorie O'Clare
Hide and Seek Copyright © 2004 Elizabeth Lapthorne
Edited by Raelene Gorlinsky, Martha Punches.
Cover art by Syneca.

This book printed in the U.S.A. by Jasmine-Jade Enterprises, LLC.

Trade paperback Publication November 2004

MAN OF HER DREAMS

ဆ

IN HER DREAMS

છ

Chapter One

ഇ

Samantha Williams squinted against the bright sun as she stepped onto the old porch of the realtor's office.

"I'm Elsa Rousseau." Her friend shook hands with an older, pot-bellied human. "We're here to see some land."

"Yes. I remember you calling." He stepped out onto the porch, wiping his hand on his faded jeans. "I'm Tommy Arnoldson. We can take my jeep, and I'll show you the old place."

Half an hour later, Samantha was being jostled in the back seat of Tommy Arnoldson's jeep. Human sweat lingered in the leather seats turning her stomach. Not even the rich smells of the countryside drowned out the odor. But she grew alert when a large, rambling house came into view.

"Is that it?" She nudged Elsa, who sat up front next to the realtor.

Elsa turned, grinning. "Yeah, isn't it awesome?"

It looked dilapidated and way too big, but Samantha nodded. "It looks great."

Samantha climbed out of the jeep after the realtor parked, and stared at the three-story house. More than one shutter appeared ready to fall off with a good wind. A wide front porch wrapped around either side of the front of the house. Their footsteps echoed as they walked across the old floorboards, worn and unsturdy, creaking while she stepped on them. The entire house was almost devoid of paint, making it impossible to determine what color it once had been. The harsh winters had weatherized the wood, giving it a natural, rustic look.

Tommy stopped and gestured with a wide swoop of his hand. "This old thing sits in the middle of a thousand acres. Over a hundred years ago, it was a rather prosperous boarding house."

Samantha watched Elsa glance inside, and then walk around the large wraparound porch.

"I'll take it." Elsa grinned at her, her happiness drowning out the smell of the human.

"Well, I'll be darned." The pudgy man clapped his thick hands and then rubbed them together. "Let's go back to my office and I'll do up some paperwork."

* * * * *

Samantha's thoughts drifted while she and Elsa drove in amiable silence. Every time Johann fucked her, touched her, entered the room she was in, her insides flip-flopped. No werewolf had ever made her crave him just by walking into a room. Even now, returning to town, knowing he was here working with Rick, made her pussy swell, her nipples harden. She couldn't think about Johann without getting wet. Damn. She had it bad for the werewolf. Really fucking bad.

Elsa pulled into the gravel parking lot of the diner where most of the pack congregated by midday. Samantha glanced around at the lack of cars.

She felt more nervous than a trapped doe when they parked in front of Harry's diner. What would Johann think? Elsa had just purchased a boarding house with her inheritance money. Rick would move the pack immediately. She had no choice but to stay with her pack; she was a single bitch.

But Johann...She wanted to be with Johann. Would he move with the pack?

"Closed?" Samantha stared at the sign hanging crooked on the glass door to the establishment. "Why would they be closed?"

"When was the last time the diner closed?" Elsa's bewilderment filled the air around them.

"It's open twenty-four hours, in case anyone wants to stop in after a run." Samantha peered through the glass, staring at the empty tables inside. "This doesn't make sense."

She turned to stare at Elsa. "I wonder where Johann is."

They both turned at the sound of popping gravel. Simone DeBeaux, the *Lunewulf* bitch who'd joined the pack when Johann had, pulled to a stop in front of them, dust from the gravel filling the air.

She rolled down her window, lifted her sunglasses and squinted at them. "Johann sent me to look for you. Everyone is over at Miranda's. Better hurry."

Her tone left no room for argument. She let her glasses drop over her nose and brushed her hair with her fingers while she drove off. Samantha stared after her, unable to stop the twinge of jealousy that ran through her. Simone had known Johann from their previous pack, both of them being *Lunewulf*. And even though Johann ignored Simone for the most part, the two of them had a cub together. She knew Johann well enough to know he would look out for his den, legitimate or not.

"Johann doesn't want her. Trust me." Elsa squeezed Samantha's arm.

She turned to search Elsa's concerned expression. "We better go find out what is going on."

Minutes later they entered through the back door at Miranda's. The smell of anger and pain flooded Samantha's senses, tying her stomach in knots. Something was wrong. Terribly wrong.

"There you are." Miranda looked up from a salve she stirred in a wooden bowl.

"I had some business to take care of. What are you making?" Elsa wrinkled her brow as she sniffed the air. "Is someone hurt?"

"You've missed some excitement." Miranda nodded toward her living room and carried the bowl in that direction.

Samantha followed Miranda and Elsa into the living room and gasped at the makeshift hospital in front of her.

"What happened?" Elsa looked at Miranda, who began covering a rather deep gash on Lyle's arm with her pink-gray poultice.

"Two rogue werewolves did this. They thought they could enter town and find themselves a piece of tail." Lyle spoke through gritted teeth as he watched his arm being wrapped in gauze.

Miranda secured the gauze near her mate's elbow. "We thought they were from Ethan Masterson's pack, you know, trying to claim the territory. But he didn't know them. They went after Rocky."

"Holy shit! Was she hurt?" Samantha looked around the room for her friend.

Elsa started helping Miranda, immediately assuming the role of queen bitch. But Samantha wanted to know where everyone was, where Johann was.

"Rocky got a little beat up I'm told. Marty is bringing her over, although I hardly know where to put them." Miranda looked around at her three patients. "I can only tend to them so fast. I guess we can put her in one of the bedrooms upstairs."

Elsa shook her head. "Let's take her over to Rick's house. There is plenty of room there."

"Where did this happen?" Samantha watched while Miranda gathered several herbs to send with Elsa.

"At the diner. Harry had to close the place. I guess Rocky was sitting at the counter and Harry was back in his office. He tried to stop the two men when they decided to help themselves to things that weren't on the menu." Once she was satisfied with the medicinal supplies to be sent with Elsa, Miranda reached for her phone. "You might as well head on out. I'll call Marty and have him tell Rick that his queen bitch is executing her rights."

Samantha chewed her lip all the way over to Rick's. She wondered where Johann was. He would go after those two rogues. No matter what Rick ordered. Johann would take matters into his own hands. But what if there were others? A sick feeling rose in her stomach at the thought of Johann getting hurt. With a new pack moving in, werewolves would test their boundaries, disregard pack leaders' orders. Anything could happen.

"Why don't you go find Johann?" Elsa patted her arm after they parked in Rick's driveway. "You'll feel much better after you do."

Samantha smiled, but she couldn't stop the dread that grew in her gut. Uneasiness rolled in the air around them. Bad times lay ahead.

Chapter Two

ക

Johann stood outside the gas station where he'd stopped to fill his tank, and listened to the two werewolves share their stories about the attack at the diner.

He glanced up at the familiar car pulling in to park. Simone hopped out, catching the attention of the werewolves with him immediately. Having grown up with her, he knew he must not see what everyone else saw. Her youth was gone, more than likely from being a single mother. He didn't like how much makeup she wore, or the cheap perfume she always seemed to douse herself with.

His mood turned sour watching her. "Did you find Samantha?"

"Yes. She and Elsa are headed over to Rick's." She held his daughter's hand, who was staring up at him with innocent sky-blue eyes. Jere was quite possibly the most beautiful cub he'd ever seen. So petite, her beautiful pale blond hair falling past her shoulders.

"Where are you headed?" he asked, wanting to take the cub in his arms, snuggle with her for just a moment.

His daughter, Jere; the daughter he'd just recently learned he had. It would take a while for him to forgive Simone for keeping her existence from him. At first, Simone hadn't known where to find him. And he had no idea he'd left her pregnant. The casual relationship had been just that. Never in his dreams would he have guessed such a beautiful cub would have come from it.

"I thought I would grab Jere a snack and then see what the pack is doing."

16

Pulling out his wallet, he handed her some money. "Let me pay for it."

She hesitated for a moment before accepting the cash. He knew she'd had it rough, struggling to make it even before her cub came along. Handouts were something new for Simone, but she would have to get accustomed to it. He would be part of his cub's life. And he would support her.

Another car pulled up, and he spotted Samantha sitting in the driver's seat. She didn't get out right away, but watched the two of them, her hesitation apparent as she chewed her lip. Excusing himself, he ruffled Jere's hair before walking over to Samantha.

Just watching her, those full red lips of hers pouting while she glanced past him at the group of werewolves, he wanted to pull her into his arms. Her blonde hair, dyed almost white and cut short around her face, was windblown. She had a self-confident look about her, but then that's what he liked about her. Samantha always seemed a bit on the cocky side. It had taken getting to know her to see that her rough exterior covered up hesitation and uncertainty.

He smiled, opening her car door for her. "Hey, sexy."

She swung her long thin legs out of the car, standing while he blocked her so she couldn't move.

"What are you doing?" She sounded irritated, jealousy lingering around her. Its stale smell didn't cover up the fact that she was also aroused.

"I was about to ask the same of you." He hadn't liked not knowing where she was when he'd heard that Rocky had been attacked at the diner. "Where have you been all morning?"

"Elsa asked me to go look at some land with her. She bought it." She gave him her attention, finally.

"Good. I'm sure the pack will be able to move soon then."

Her tongue darted out, running over her lips. His cock hardened just watching the small action. He knew all too well what that mouth was capable of. Those full lips, so soft. He ran his thumb over them, enjoying how her eyes darkened to a dark brown.

"I don't like not knowing where you are," he whispered, moving closer.

The car door blocked them from Jere's view. He pressed against her, his insides tightening while his blood raced through him straight to his cock. Just touching her brought out every predatory instinct in him. He wanted to mark every inch of her — *mine*. But she always looked so hesitant, almost shying away from him.

"I'm not that hard to find." Defiance appeared in her expression. She pursed her lips, narrowing her gaze on him. "It's a small pack."

"And it was attacked today. If I'd known where you were, I wouldn't have worried."

Everything in her expression softened, a small smile tempting her lips. It would take time to make her see that she answered to him now. Samantha had been on her own most of her life, running with several different packs. It wouldn't be that way for her anymore, not if he had anything to say about it.

"Don't you think I can take care of myself?" Samantha always had to show her tough side.

He didn't buy it for a moment. "Not against an entire pack."

She didn't discuss a lot of her past with him. But he knew a single bitch running on her own faced the threat of being attacked by a pack of werewolves up to no good. Her cheeks flushed. She understood what he implied.

But she had nothing to worry about. He would protect her. He wanted to protect her. Reaching for her, brushing his fingers over the flush in her cheeks, feeling her heat, he knew he would kill for her.

Pressing against her, he kissed her. The heat from her mouth spread through him like wildfire, igniting faster than he could control it. His cock hardened to the point of pain inside his jeans. He pulled her closer, wrapping his arms around her while he devoured her mouth like a madman.

She didn't fight him, made no attempt to slow the kiss. And that was what he adored about her, among so many things. No matter where they were, she never stopped his advances, never suggested their behavior wasn't proper. Samantha had a sexual appetite that was endless. She always wanted him as badly as he wanted her.

"If you fuck her right here in the parking lot, can I watch?" Simone's sultry chuckle grated on his nerves.

Taking a deep breath, he pressed Samantha to him, not wanting to see the irritation on her face. He felt it enough for both of them. Looking over her at the car parked next to Samantha's, he glared at Simone. She'd managed to walk past them without him noticing, and had just shut the car door after securing Jere in the back seat.

"Go over to Rick's house and see what you can do to help," he told her.

She straightened, ready to tell him to go to hell, he imagined. But then without answering, she turned and got into her car.

Looking down at Samantha, he saw the question in her eyes. She didn't understand that he had an obligation to Simone. As sire to her cub, he would have to take care of her too, until he could find a suitable mate for her. Werewolves took care of their own.

"I need to fuck you." He would show her what it meant to be taken care of. All the explanations in the world wouldn't work as well as showing her. "Follow me back to my room."

She nodded, once again licking those adorable full lips of hers.

Pulling into one of the parking spaces in front of the Inn where he was staying, he waited for Samantha to join him. He took her hand, her warm skin so soft to touch.

"I want you in my mouth," she whispered, while he unlocked the door.

His fingers shook, and she giggled when he couldn't unlock the door right away.

He pulled her into the room, shutting the door behind them. "You want me to fuck your face, baby?"

"Oh yes." She smiled up at him, her fingers dancing around his cock while she fumbled with his zipper.

His heart pounded blood straight to his cock, the pressure building so fiercely he worried he would explode before she could release him. She smiled but the slight tremble he saw creep through her drove him wild. Samantha could hardly wait to get to his cock.

She went down on her knees in front of him, not bothering to shed her clothes, or even go to the bed. His cock finally freed, her tongue darted around it, moist heat rushing through him fast enough to make his head spin.

"I love how you taste." Her breath washed over the sensitive skin on his shaft, while her fingers held him like a cherished gift.

She was gentle and rough all at the same time. Stroking him with her hand, she guided him into her mouth, her lips soft while her tongue lashed at him, offering no mercy.

"Dear God, woman." He could smell her desire. He loved how sucking his cock turned her on.

She moaned, vibrations caressing him while chills raced through him. Johann ran his hands over her hair, gripping her head, while he began slow, controlled movements in and out of her mouth. She let go of his shaft and ran her hands up his chest, submitting completely to him while he fucked her face.

Her lips stretched around his cock, over half of him disappearing into her mouth, and then sliding out over those full, luscious lips. Her eyelids fluttered and then she looked up at him. Long eyelashes draped over her glazed stare.

"You are so beautiful," he murmured.

She answered him with an evil dance of her tongue around his shaft.

"Fuck." A growl escaped before he could stop it. Electric currents darted through him where her fingertips grazed over his chest.

He could feel her heat, smell her lust; the fire burning from her mouth surged through him, awakening the beast inside him. Blood pumped faster through his veins, his heart racing in his chest, almost painfully. A wonderful erotic pain. Holding her head, he thrust deep inside her mouth, feeling her throat tighten around him. He would spill his seed in her mouth if he wasn't careful.

Working to focus, he stared down at her. Her eyes had closed. She would endure all he would give her. But he wanted her to enjoy this, too. Samantha could scream in pleasure, and those sounds carried him through the day. He wanted to hear her pleasure, see her lust satisfied on her face, watch her body spasm with joy.

Pulling his cock from her mouth, he enjoyed her dazed expression before reaching for her, lifting her up.

"Fuck me," she whispered, and he wanted nothing more than to do just that.

He watched her remove her clothes, her hands trembling while she pulled her shirt over her head. Large breasts almost fell out of her bra, the lacy material no match for the full soft mounds. He cupped them, squeezing them together, wanting desperately to place his cock deep between their fullness.

She unbuttoned her jeans, smiling up at him with such eagerness his body ached for her.

"Come here, wolf man." She slid out of her jeans, leaving them as a puddle on the floor while she backed up toward his bed. "Fuck me. Hurry."

He stepped out of his jeans as well, then pulled his t-shirt off with little effort. Climbing over her, he spread her long thin legs, the scent of her pussy drowning him like a rich sweet drug. The heat of her cunt reached his cock before he touched her. But when he pressed against her moist folds, he could hardly breathe. Lust hung so thick in the air he drowned in it, unable to focus on anything but being deep inside her.

"You asked for it, little bitch." He gritted his teeth, feeling the pressure grow in him while his beast's cravings battled to take over.

He drove into her, filling her instantly. She slid across the bed, reaching for him, her nails dragging over his skin while she cried out.

"Shit. Oh—fuck." She clung to him, her eyes wide as her mouth formed an adorable circle.

"This is what you want, isn't it?" He pulled out of her, feeling her thick cream cling to him while her muscles contracted around him.

"Yes," she managed to gasp, and then clawed at the air when he drove into her again.

He knelt on his haunches, spreading her legs, her perfumed lust filling the air. Burying himself deep inside her again, her heat tormenting him, feeding his lust. He pounded her cunt, feeling his come swell inside him. He wouldn't be able to hold out much longer. But she felt so damned good. Her silky-smooth muscles wrapped around him, sucking him deeper inside her. If he could only hold out, enjoy being inside her just a few more minutes...

"Samantha, I..." Everything inside him begged to explode. He struggled to bury himself just a bit deeper, relish in her pleasure for one more second.

Her heat suffocated him, her muscles clamping down so hard, demanding his climax. Johann let go, releasing his hot fluid. Her muscles trembled around his cock while she went over the edge with him.

"Damn," she breathed, reaching for him, pulling him over her, wrapping her arms and legs around him, holding him inside her. "You are so awesome, Johann."

He smiled, hearing her satisfaction. Rolling to his back, he nestled her on top of him. The pack would call for them soon enough. But until they did, he wanted nothing more than to be alone with Samantha.

As he stroked her back, she relaxed over him, her heart slowing its beat against his chest. It didn't take long before he knew she'd fallen asleep. His thoughts strayed to what might lay ahead of them. An adventure. A new home. And although both of them had known a lot of running, jumping from one pack to the other, this time they would do it together. Or at least he hoped she would stay with him.

Chapter Three

Ꙃ

Samantha woke up slowly to the phone ringing.

"It's four o'clock in the morning. Who would be calling at this hour?" She stared at the glowing numbers on the clock radio. The phone next to it rang again.

Johann reached over her and grabbed the phone before it rang a third time. Samantha untangled herself from twisted covers. Her legs were wobbly when she stood, rich cream saturated her inner thighs. Her pussy throbbed, and she turned to stare at Johann's gorgeous body, the sheet barely covering the thick muscles that rippled under his skin.

"Hello," he said into the phone, while reaching for her, stroking her pussy with one finger. Fire ignited inside her instantly.

"What's going on?" She opened her eyes when he pulled his fingers away, wondering why he had stopped.

"Get dressed. We're headed over to Rick's house." His tone made her stomach sink. The pack had endured an attack earlier. Now what had happened?

Fortunately, humans weren't nocturnal. The roads were isolated, making the trip across town take only minutes. Several other cars were parked in the driveway at Rick's when they arrived, and Samantha heard voices in the kitchen before they entered through the back door.

Rocky, Rick's cousin, stood talking with Elsa while she made coffee. Elsa's worried expression faded noticeably when she saw Johann.

"I'm so glad you're here." She walked into his arms, hugging him before reaching for Samantha, offering her a reassuring smile.

Samantha ran her fingers through her hair, certain it was disheveled. Worry hung so thick in the air she could hardly breathe.

"Where's Rick?" Johann asked, releasing Elsa.

In the next second, Marty and Toby, two other packmates, strolled through the back door, their expressions grim. Marty pulled Rocky into his arms, kissing the curls on top of her head.

"Is it true?" Rocky whispered.

"Is what true?" Samantha wrapped her arms around her waist, hugging herself.

Everyone looked sick with worry, while tension filled the air. Rick entered the kitchen from the living room, the disgustingly sweet smell of outrage needling the air around him.

"It sounds like it's true." Rick put his arm around Elsa possessively, heavy worry lines under his eyes when he glanced at everyone in the kitchen. "We've got a run going on. And it's another pack—not good."

"A run?" Samantha couldn't hide her alarm and stepped back, pressing against Johann. He wrapped his arms around her waist.

"Is it the Duluth pack?" Johann asked, holding her close to him. She could feel his heart pounding against her back. His anger filled the air around them.

"Yup. We got word down at the bar that they're coming through and claiming the territory." Marty's expression was chiseled in stone.

Everyone in the room turned their attention to Rick, waiting for his instructions.

"How many are there?" Rick's grip tightened around Elsa, and Samantha watched her stroke his arm. She knew he feared the worst.

"Man, I'm not sure." Marty had pulled Rocky up to his chest.

She rested against him and Samantha could see tears welling in her eyes.

"There are enough that they've drawn the attention of the local police department," Marty continued. "That's how we heard of it—can you believe it—it was on the TV. Some kids partying south of town spotted them heading this direction. Scared the shit out of them from what was reported on the news."

"Dammit." Rick's arm muscles flexed noticeably. "The last thing we need are humans in a panic."

"Ethan Masterson is taking over the territory." Marty's voice sounded a bit more garbled than it had a second before. Teeth bulged against his lips. "But if he isn't careful, he will make it so that no werewolves can live here."

Tears fell down Elsa's cheek and Johann reached for a napkin on the counter. He handed it to her, her smile fading quickly when Rick growled. Samantha felt the room spin around her, the air too clogged with emotions. She knew Rick didn't like Johann. Elsa and Johann had grown up in the same pack. In fact, Elsa's pack had tried to make her mate with Johann. If Rick wouldn't accept Johann, would he move with the pack? What if Rick chased him off? Her mouth suddenly felt drier than sandpaper. She didn't want to leave with the pack without Johann.

Johann let go of Samantha, squaring his shoulders as he faced Rick. The room grew deathly silent.

"I'm here to help. You need werewolf power, and you can count me in. If you'll have me." Johann didn't seem to notice, or he intentionally ignored, the hardened look their pack leader gave him.

Rick let a moment pass before answering, his tone no more than a growl. "I'll take your help — if that is in fact why you are here."

Samantha wanted to cry. Her heart pounded so hard against her ribs that it hurt. Rick had taken her in, given her a home, and treated her with respect even though she'd been a single bitch out running on her own. Most packs shunned such a woman, whispering atrocities about her whether they were true or not. But Rick hadn't done that, and she'd been appreciative of him giving her a chance to show she wasn't a slut.

And she just couldn't believe that Johann wanted Elsa. She'd seen no signs of it. She wanted to jump in between the two werewolves and yell at them to stop thinking with their cocks. Emotions ran strong at the moment, but they were all on the same side.

"Rick. He is here to help the pack — nothing else." Elsa turned to face her mate, her long blond hair streaming down her back.

Rick nodded, wrapping his arms around Elsa, but giving Johann a hard look before turning his attention to the others in the room. The phone rang, and Elsa pulled free to answer it.

"Everyone might as well get comfortable in the living room. I'm sure we'll have the whole pack here before long." Rick stood to the side, allowing the others to stream out of the kitchen.

Johann reached for Samantha taking her hand before following everyone else into the other room. He gestured to the couch, and she sat down, disappointed when he moved to stand against the wall. She would have to turn to see him, and didn't want to make a fool out of herself by gawking at the werewolf she knew she was falling in love with.

Tension ran thick through the air, but she couldn't stop dwelling on her own fears. Johann was an alpha male. She saw that. And she was definitely attracted to him because of it. But a pack couldn't have too many alphas. And if one existed who wasn't pack leader, he had to learn to submit, or leave. She doubted Johann would be able to submit. But if he left, would he take her with him?

Johann had a strong pedigree. His *Lunewulf* heritage ran thick for generations. She had *Lunewulf* blood in her, but the breed frowned even more on half-breeds than they did on American werewolves. She had nothing to offer him. Nothing but herself.

And she had given all of herself to him.

Everyone chatted quietly around her, but she focused on her hands, remembering how she had touched Johann. Her fingers tingled when she pictured his smooth skin, bulging muscles rippling underneath, moving when she ran her hands over them. The dark hair on his chest tickled when he had pressed against her. Her nipples hardened at the thought.

Her inner thighs still ached from when he had held her legs, keeping them spread wide while he'd fucked her. Closing her eyes, she had a clear picture of watching his cock disappear inside her. When he pulled out, her thick white cream covered his shaft. Her pussy throbbed at the thought.

She remembered the look of determination on his face, his teeth gritted while he pounded her. A hint of silver would swirl in his blue eyes when he fucked her, the beast within him threatening to take over. Their lovemaking was so primal, so raw, so perfect.

But that wasn't all that made Johann the catch of a lifetime. Here he was, with a pack that stood in jeopardy, in a home where the pack leader was moments from attacking him. Johann would take on a challenge. He didn't shy away from danger. Now if she could only get him to commit to her.

Rick entered the living room, his angry scent grabbing her attention. There were people on his couch, sitting on the floor, and leaning against the wall. Samantha jumped up when Elsa entered so she could sit down. Rick stood behind her as he addressed his small pack.

"I don't have to tell any of you that we have an uphill battle ahead of us." He let out a large sigh and looked around at the somber faces staring back at him. "Our pack has existed for six generations in northern Minnesota. We fought hard to establish our hunting grounds and we have damn good land to feed us."

"That's why Masterson wants our land." Harry spoke up after plopping down on the corner of the couch next to Elsa.

"I'd say they're after more than hunting ground." Johann glanced over at Rocky. "They want your bitches, too."

Several loud outbursts followed. Marty jumped in front of Rocky and Rick moved quickly to get between him and Johann.

"We won't be able to defend our territory worth a damn if all we do is fight among ourselves. Masterson said those werewolves weren't part of his pack." Rick finally got everyone into his or her seats. "Either way, Masterson's pack outnumbers ours and I fear Ramona fed him more information about our pack than any of us wants to believe."

"And up until recently, some of us felt free to interact with their pack." Miranda looked pointedly at Samantha.

Several of the bitches had run freely with the Duluth pack in the past. Rocky had invited her to run with the pack several days after she'd arrived here.

"And I didn't have a problem with that," Rick was quick to point out.

"Their pack has some nice tails we chased after a time or too," someone yelled out and immediately more comments flew.

Samantha looked around trying to follow the conversation, but everyone started talking over one another again. She looked up when Rick yelled for silence.

"Folks, we need to stay focused here. We have a pack headed this way. The local law will slow them down somewhat, but we all know they won't be able to stop them." Rick had everyone's attention now.

"If this pack is trying to run us out of town, they won't care if they kill a few humans. It will bring the heat down on us, not them," Marty added quickly.

"Right. The four of us." Rick gestured with his hand to include himself, Marty, Toby, and Johann. "We'll head out to the edge of our hunting ground and see what direction this run is headed."

"I can help," Lyle piped up.

"Me too," Harry added. "Millie is willing to have her two sons help out. She has several folks at the Inn so she can't shut down for the night."

Rick shook his head. "I'll make sure Millie is told thanks, but we can't risk our young ones. Her boys can help run errands if we need it, but I don't want them out on a run."

Elsa nodded her agreement silently and Rick rested his hand on her shoulder.

"All right, let's head out."

The sun rested on the horizon by the time everyone was settled. Rocky and Samantha sat at the kitchen table when Elsa trotted down the stairs.

"I'm sure the men will be back soon." Samantha got up to start more coffee while Elsa sat down to brush out her damp hair.

"I'll make a large breakfast." Elsa put the brush down and began searching through the cabinets and refrigerator to see what was on hand.

Samantha watched Elsa search the kitchen. "I have an idea."

"What are you going to do?" Rocky watched warily while Samantha slipped her shoes off.

"I'm going to get some fish. It's not that far away to the nearest lake. I'm sure I can outrun any of that Duluth pack anyway. I do have some *Lunewulf* blood in me." Samantha slipped her sweater off and walked to the door.

"Johann could catch you," Rocky said with a giggle.

Elsa twisted her hair behind her back. "I think he's already caught her."

"I sure hope you're right about that one." Samantha wagged her eyebrows, determined to look confident so her friends wouldn't worry. "I'll be right back."

Chapter Four

∞

Samantha opened the broiler and sniffed the wonderful aroma of the cooking trout. Elsa stacked hot biscuits onto a plate. Several hours had passed since Samantha had returned with the fish and she wondered when the men would show up. The sun was well into the sky and no werewolf was safe in his fur during daylight hours. Their delay meant only one thing. They had traveled further north to burn their dead.

"Here they come." Rocky peered out the back window and turned to the door as the men ambled in from the cold.

Elsa looked at the forlorn men and quickly took charge. "Samantha, make sure there are fresh towels in the bathroom. Rocky, run over to your place and do the same. Marty and Toby, you can shower over there. Johann, you can shower here once Rick is through. As soon as you're clean, there's plenty of food ready to eat."

"Go on upstairs." Rick nodded to Johann. He then turned his attention to Elsa, telling her about two of the pack members who were killed when they took on some of the Duluth pack.

Samantha saw her friend's tears and knew she should comfort her, or help contact the dens. Miranda had stepped in, and Elsa cuddled into Rick's arms. Suddenly feeling awkward, she turned her attention to Johann.

He looked tired, his hair streaked with blood and sweat. There were scratches on his arms, and his clothes were wrinkled and damp, more than likely from being left in a pile outside while they fought the other pack. He didn't look her way, but turned toward the stairs, running grass-stained fingers through his hair.

She hesitated for a minute before following him, stopping again when she reached the stairs. Maybe she shouldn't go after him if he needed time alone.

Halfway up the stairs Johann turned, looking down at her. His expression still looked torn, sorrow and anger mixing with the smell of sweat and something earthy. He studied her for just a moment, but her heart constricted during that time. She should have left him alone, not followed him. She was being a pest.

He reached for her, extending his hand. "Come," he said, and she was up the stairs before she thought about it.

Murder wasn't part of a werewolf's nature. She didn't know what Johann had witnessed, or what he had done, but she wouldn't press him to talk. He held her hand, leading the way to the bathroom at the top of the stairs. Closing the door behind them, he pulled off her shirt before taking off his own clothes. She continued to strip while he started the water.

Johann pulled her into the hot shower with him, still not speaking. Instead, he wrapped his arms around her, holding her securely against him, almost to the point where she couldn't breathe.

Steam drifted around them, thick with the smells of their bodies, and their lust. Johann's heart pounded against her chest, the muscles in his arms tightening and relaxing. Whatever demons coursed through his body, she would give him this time. Relaxing in his arms, she hoped he would see that she was there for him. She supported him. Dammit to hell. She loved him.

"Turn around," he growled, at the same time taking her arms, and turning her so her back was to him. "I need inside you."

Samantha's heart skipped a beat, then started pounding furiously. She pressed her palms against the shower wall, arching her back while his hands caressed her. Water streamed down her skin, her hair sticking to her face. She closed her eyes, her insides tightening when he grabbed her ass.

His hard cock pressed against her, pressing first against her ass, then pushing down further toward her cunt. Excitement rushed through her. The thought of fucking in someone else's home, in their shower, made her heart beat even faster.

"Your pussy is so hot." He pushed his cock toward her hole, her folds swelling with need.

"I want you in me. Please. Johann." She tried to look over her shoulder, to see his face, but water sprayed off his shoulder, blinding her.

"Like this baby?" He shoved, and in spite of the water rushing over her, moisture soaked her cunt, allowing him to dive deep inside her with his first thrust.

"Yes. Hell, yes." She braced herself to maintain her balance against his thrust.

He had aimed deep, and with the angle just right, impaled her fully when he entered her. She stifled a cry, doing her best to keep from making too much noise in their pack leader's home. Johann spread her ass, the hot water trickling down her, teasing her while he moved slowly in and out of her.

"You're always so tight," he breathed, kneading her rear end, gripping and squeezing, his breath growing louder with each thrust.

She leaned against the shower wall, pressing her cheek against its coolness. Pressure built inside her with each thrust, the water washing free her cream while it dribbled down between them. It made her feel so clean, his cock bringing to life every nerve ending inside her. She could feel every movement, his muscles contracting, his shaft sliding in and out of her.

A dam of desire within her threatened to break, releasing a flow of passion and almost unbearable pressure.

"Johann. I..." She almost told him she loved him. But those words hadn't been spoken, and she couldn't bring herself to ruin the moment if he didn't love her, too.

"Come for me, Samantha." He slid his hands to her hips, pulling her back while he continued to thrust forward. "I'm going to explode inside you."

"Yes. Oh, yes." His movements were rough, his grip hard, the water splashed off of them while he moved faster and faster.

Heat surged through her, his cock hit just the right spot to send electric currents flying through her. Arching her back as far as she could, encouraging his penetration to go as deep as possible, the pressure exploded inside her, wave after wave rushing through her while her orgasm seemed to rip her in two.

Johann made one final thrust, wrapping his arms around her, burying himself deep inside her. She relished in the hot sensation that coated her pussy, knowing his seed squirted deep into her womb. For a moment, she wished she weren't on birth control. Surely such an intense act would cause conception. But their relationship wasn't at that level. And she had no idea if it would ever get there.

The water hit her at a different angle, not quite as hot as it was when they first got in the shower. Johann continued to hold her while he straightened, his cock slowly sliding out of her but resting in the crack of her rear end, hard, hot and still throbbing.

For a long moment he didn't move, but kept her wrapped in his arms, holding on to her like she was his lifeline. Or at least she imagined that was what he was doing. She knew in reality he was a strong enough man that he didn't need her to lean on. But for that moment, she enjoyed resting her back against his chest, his muscular arms crossing between her breasts. Cuddling into him like this seemed like the safest place in the world.

"Let me wash you before the water gets cold," she whispered, hating to end the moment, but knowing others needed to shower too.

He relaxed his grip, allowing her to turn in his arms. Without looking up at him, she reached for the soap and washcloth, created lather, and began stroking his soft skin that covered his solid protruding muscles. She washed every inch of him, taking care to remove all grass and mud stains from his body. By the time she'd finished, they rinsed in tepid water.

Samantha could see Rick standing in his bedroom when she walked out of the bathroom. Steam filled the air around her, and she knew their lust saturated the moist air. He turned his attention to her, his masked expression unreadable.

"Go downstairs," Johann said from behind her. "I need to talk to Rick."

"I'll make you a plate of food." She turned to look at him, but Johann had his attention on Rick, his expression just as unreadable.

There wasn't a scrap of food left when everyone started to mingle in the living room. Johann was one of the last to enter the room, wiping remnants of food from his mouth while he approached her.

Rick paced on the other side of the room behind Elsa, who sat in a rocking chair talking quietly to Miranda. Both women looked up toward Rick when he cleared his throat.

"I think we proved today that we aren't large enough to defend our territory." Rick seemed to watch the expression on everyone's face carefully. No one said a word. "We lost two good men today—two men in their prime. I won't lose any more of you to a battle we won't be able to win in the end. I've decided we're going to meet with the Duluth pack leader, make a formal announcement, and then we're moving. I plan to move quickly on this so if you need to give notice at your jobs than I suggest you do it."

"Rick, this is our land," Marty interrupted. "Our parents fought for this territory. Your dad led our pack and ruled this territory. Are you sure about this?"

"I haven't opened the floor for discussion. This is how it's going to be. Are you questioning me as pack leader?"

Samantha turned to look at Johann, who sat on the edge of the couch next to her. She saw an expression on his face she hadn't seen before. His features might as well have been chiseled from stone. Not a muscle on his face moved. His blue eyes were darker than a thunderhead ready to explode. He didn't take his gaze off Marty.

"Man, you know I'm not...and that's not what I meant by what I said." Marty sat next to Rocky on the floor. He looked relaxed, but his expression was serious. "I just wondered if we couldn't try to reason with Masterson."

"I plan to call him. In fact, I thought I might do that tonight. I'm going to let him know that we're moving—and to give us a month or so before they move in." Rick remained standing and he looked at everyone in the room.

Samantha glanced around at the others in the room. Everyone seemed to be squirming in his or her seats, but no one said a thing. Nor did anyone make eye contact with Rick. She knew Rick's words didn't sit well with any of them. Admitting defeat, backing down without a fight...these weren't traits of a werewolf. She understood why Rick made the decision he did. She could only imagine how difficult the decision to retreat had been for him.

She wanted to reach out to Johann. She wanted to know what he thought of all of this. Not once had he commented to her either way whether he supported Rick's decisions or not.

Samantha didn't pay much attention to the rest of the meeting. She sat next to Johann and leaned back in the couch. She was aware of his leg brushing against hers from time to time. It simply aided in reminding her how powerful he was...and the expression that appeared on his face when

Marty questioned Rick left no doubt that he was willing to use that power. Somehow, that thought sent a warm rush through her body. She ached to fuck him again already.

Chapter Five

ഇ

Everyone congregated around the front door after the meeting. Several left right away, needing to get home and shower before heading out to work. Two-week notices would be given out today. The pack was preparing to leave town.

Samantha helped carry empty glasses and coffee mugs to the kitchen. Rocky stood in there alone, staring out the back door. She turned when Samantha put the dishes in the sink.

"It's a beautiful sunrise," she murmured.

Samantha thought she still looked a bit pale. "How are you feeling?"

Rocky shrugged, an attempt at a smile playing at her lips. "They grabbed me, but they didn't get away with much."

Marty lumbered in, his size filling the kitchen. Agitation swarmed around him although he offered Rocky an impish grin. "I would have been mad if you had already left." He winked at Samantha.

"Oh, yeah?" Rocky moved into his arms, a rosy pallor spreading across her cheeks. "I'm not going anywhere without you."

Their easy affection for each other was enviable.

"Come with me while I run over to my apartment," Marty rumbled into Rocky's hair.

Elsa entered, carrying more coffee mugs, with Johann at her side. Apparently he'd just said something to make her laugh. Her pretty blue eyes sparkled as she looked up at him. He playfully tugged at her long blonde hair.

Rocky turned to look at Elsa. "Do you need me around here to help you with anything?"

"If you feel okay, I don't see why you can't go if you want." Elsa gave her friend the once over.

Rocky glanced at Samantha, and then at Elsa. Rocky had led a fairly sheltered life thanks to her older cousin, Rick, being pack leader, and his father pack leader before him. The wild look in Rocky's eyes outraged Samantha. Rocky was damned lucky she hadn't been raped.

"Physically I feel fine, but look..." Rocky held a shaking hand out, standing in between Samantha and Elsa, so the others couldn't see.

"Then go," Elsa whispered. "I think Marty wants to take care of you."

Samantha sensed the worry surrounding Elsa, but her calm tone made Rocky smile. Elsa would make a good queen bitch. She handled the situation well. Samantha would have wanted to find those brutes and kick some ass.

"I know he does." Rocky couldn't stop the blush that started at her neck and quickly spread to her cheekbones.

Rocky hugged each of them before cuddling into Marty and letting him guide her out the back door.

She turned before leaving. "Samantha? Would you like to stay with me tonight?"

"Sure." Samantha reached out, squeezing Rocky's hand.

"Good idea." Marty nodded his approval, and then led Rocky out the door.

Samantha would have preferred staying with Johann, but her friend needed her. And at least if Johann didn't suggest she stay the night, she wouldn't have to pace in her small apartment wondering where he was. It would do him good knowing she wasn't always at his beck and call. If he wanted to see her, he would have to go to Rocky's.

"Elsa." Rick appeared in the doorway. "Simone is on the phone. She wants to talk to you."

Elsa had just started rinsing dishes. "Tell her just a minute."

"Do you want me to talk to her?" Johann stood behind Rick, his attention on Elsa with a gentle expression he seemed to reserve for whenever he talked to her.

Samantha studied him for a moment, knowing he would do anything for Elsa. But she realized that his compassion for Elsa was brotherly. She caught Rick's gaze, dark and speculative as he watched her. She looked away, turning her attention to Elsa.

"I can rinse the dishes for you," she suggested. "Go see what she wants."

She would rather Elsa talk to Simone than Johann. She'd never seen him give Simone a brotherly look.

Elsa tossed the dishcloth to Samantha. "Help yourself," she smiled, and then headed toward the phone.

Rick turned to follow her, while Johann moved to the side, allowing the two of them to pass. Samantha watched him look into Rick's face when they brushed past each other. She hated that she couldn't read his expression. When he stepped into the kitchen, shifting his focus to her, she thought she smelled irritation.

"Will you always do your best to keep me from Simone?" He moved behind her, his breath hot against her neck.

Heat rushed through her, embarrassment burning her cheeks that he'd found her so obvious. But the smell of him so close made her insides feverish with lust. She ran one of the coffee mugs under the water, her hands suddenly clammy in spite of the dishwater.

"Probably," she muttered, seeing no point in trying to dodge the truth.

Johann chuckled, wrapping his arms around her waist and nibbling on her neck. She was suddenly soaked, need for him consuming her to the point where she could hardly think straight.

41

"You have nothing to worry about," he growled, tickling the sensitive skin at the nape of her neck.

"I'd better not." She flicked dishwater at him with her fingers, suddenly feeling bold.

Looking over her shoulder, she couldn't look away from his dark, possessive gaze. She could see so much in those deep blue eyes. Confidence and a touch of arrogance, knowledge and strength. The strong outline of his jawbone, his expression etched in stone, with blonde curls bordering his face that almost gave him a boyish look. All of that made him just about the sexiest werewolf she'd ever laid eyes on.

"Getting possessive on me?" His hands stroked her sides, barely touching her breasts as he moved down until his grip rested on her hips.

She fought off a shudder, his touch sending the heat swarming through her straight to her pussy. The flushed heat hadn't left her cheeks, and she looked down, hurrying to finish the dishes. She knew rejection, had experienced it more times in her life than she cared to remember. It was so unclear to her where this relationship was headed that she couldn't stand it. But she wouldn't let him see her insecurities, or her fears. Open herself up and all she would be doing was inviting in the pain.

"I see something I like, and I go after it." She reached for the last coffee mug, suddenly anxious to get out of there. "I'm no different than you."

Johann chuckled. Backing away from her he gave her rear end a sharp slap.

"Ouch. What was that for?" Tingles raced through her. The spot where his hand had smacked her rear burned slightly, but she loved the feeling.

"Because I felt like it." That boyish charm that she knew probably got him anything he wanted when he was younger seeped through.

She shut off the water, wringing the washcloth and then laying it over the edge of the sink. Turning, she held out her wet hands toward him and he grabbed her wrists, pulling her to him while he pinned her hands behind her.

"What do you feel like doing now?" she asked. Hopefully he would want her with him after they left Rick and Elsa's.

Elsa's scent reached her at the same time that Johann looked over her head. He let her go, and she turned to see Elsa staring at them, a frown on her face.

"Did Simone upset you?" Johann moved toward Elsa, but stopped when Rick entered the kitchen.

Elsa glanced at him but then turned around and reached for Rick. She wrapped her arms around Rick, but smiled at Johann.

"No. Not at all." The worry didn't leave her eyes when she glanced at Samantha. "She wants me to watch Jere. And she wanted to make sure everything was okay."

Samantha saw Johann tighten, his muscles hardening under his clothes. He wanted to know why Simone wanted a babysitter.

"We'll get out of your hair." Johann looked at Samantha when he spoke. He pulled his gaze away from her finally and his expression changed as he studied Elsa. "Don't worry so much about things. The pack supports Rick's decision to move, and will go where he says. All you need to focus on now is getting everyone ready to go."

Rick nodded contemplatively, indicating he agreed. Maybe the two werewolves would be able to get along. The last thing their pack needed right now was more trouble.

Chapter Six

Johann sucked in the morning air, more than relieved to be out of Bolton's house. The werewolf had his good points, Johann would acknowledge that, but he still managed to get on his nerves. Elsa loved him though, so Johann would put up with him. But that was the only reason.

After running with the pack, realizing how small they were, and then losing two werewolves to the Masterson pack, he knew major changes needed to take place soon. And not only with the pack. He needed to make some decisions, too.

"Let's go for a run." He turned in time to see the surprised look on Samantha's face. "Scared to take a run when the sun is coming up?"

"Are you daring me?" She was so beautiful when he challenged her, pushed her to be the incredible woman that she was.

"Nope." He walked toward his truck then opened the passenger door for her.

Her bleached blonde hair was still damp from their shower, and her skin had a rosy blush to it. She climbed into the truck, her long thin legs accented nicely in her jeans.

Driving out of town, he parked his truck at a rest stop. Clouds passed over the rising sun, adding shade to the area.

Sitting for a minute, he listened to the chatter of the birds outside. Peaceful and relaxed. There were no humans around. No one to cause them any grief. He turned his attention to Samantha, smelling her nervousness. But when she looked at him she smiled, her look determined. She would run with him because he wanted her to. Her loyalties lay with him. And that was what he needed to know.

Rick Bolton had taken her in when other packs had shunned her. He knew a bit about her past, that she'd been cast off from her den at an early age, that her lineage had made her an outcast. *Lunewulves* were snobs. His pack had made a big mistake in letting such a strong, beautiful woman like Samantha run. But their mistake was his gain.

"Let's go before the sun gets much higher." He opened his car door, standing and then pulling his shirt off. He stripped completely, tossing his clothes in his truck.

Moving around the truck, he enjoyed watching Samantha stretch while she peeled off her shirt. He moved around her when she bent over to slip out of her jeans. Taking her clothes, he tossed them in his truck as well.

"Where are we headed?" she asked.

He had no direction planned. There were decisions to make, and several werewolves relied on what he decided. He had to discuss things with Samantha and Simone. And he had to make sure he made the best choices for Jere. He would not let that little cub out of his life again. Hell. The child barely knew him. And he planned to change that. The best thing to do when options weighed heavy in his thoughts was to run, allowing the primal side of him to cleanse him. After that, his thinking would be clearer.

He allowed the change to ripple through him, blood accelerating through his veins while his bones altered their shape. Fur covered his naked body, his arms shortening and moving forward. His legs bent, no longer strong enough for him to stand on them. Dropping to all fours he sniffed the air. It was the perfect morning for a run.

Samantha dropped to all fours next to him, her petite size and glossy white coat that matched his; a dead giveaway that *Lunewulf* blood surged through her veins. But she had silver streaks, beautiful strokes of silver that proved she wasn't pure blood. In her fur she was the most erotic creature he'd ever seen.

Circling her, consuming her scent, he brushed alongside her, then tasted her. Licking her face he knew that even in their fur, he couldn't keep away from her. The little bitch had gotten into his senses, her adoring look captivating him.

She nipped at him, wagging her long sleek white tail friskily, and then took off running. She'd been blessed with the speed of the *Lunewulf*. But she was smaller than him, and he had no problem keeping up with her.

So you want to play, do you? He barked and sped past her, allowing himself the freedom to run without care, even if for just a bit.

His nature took on the primal side of him. The carnal, rawer instincts taking over while they ran. Samantha had no problem keeping up with him, although he kept a close eye on her. If there were other werewolves out here, he would kill anyone who got too close to her.

And she seemed aware of that fact. Samantha glowed with contentment; her silver eyes squinted against the wind, while she panted. Her sleek coat covered her slim figure, rippling while she kept up the pace.

They slowed at the first of the lakes in the area. Again he sniffed the air, making sure no one was around who could bother them. A flock of geese took to air as soon as they noticed the two dangerous predators invading their sanctuary. Samantha skipped into the water, lapping at it, making no attempt to be quiet. She was at peace, and he willingly stood guard, allowing her this time to relax and have no worries. When she looked up at him, her coat soaked around her mouth, she appeared to be laughing.

Dear God. She was beautiful. His cock hardened just watching her.

Glancing around again, checking the direction of the wind, and assuring they were alone, he knew they couldn't stay out too long. The sun rose higher, the warmth soaking through his thick hide, making him pant. Daylight hours weren't safe for a werewolf, not in their fur.

But this time was necessary for both of them. In their human form, emotions were suppressed, feelings kept at bay. Taking on their animal form allowed everything to even out, a soul cleansing. And with the times ahead of them, they both needed this respite.

Samantha strolled out of the water, strutting around him. Her scent consumed him while he looked down at her, knowing what she wanted.

We can't fuck during the daylight, little bitch. He growled at her actions, nipping at her when she tried to lick his cock.

Had enough for one day, wolf man? Her teasing yelps created a smoldering fire between his hind legs. He would have difficulty running if she kept up her teasing.

Lowering his head so they saw eye-to-eye, he growled a low warning. Her ears flattened and she backed down instantly. Everything was so much simpler in their fur. He ruled and she submitted. No explanations needed. It was a law that was centuries old.

Samantha nuzzled up to him, cuddling while she brushed into his side. He could fuck her right here so easily, mount her and ride her without a thought. Pressure built inside him, urging him to do just that. Without thought, he pushed her tail to the side, tasting the sweet moisture that already started to saturate her coat.

Instantly she dropped down on her front legs, sticking her adorable ass in the air, preparing for him. Never had this woman told him no, not in her skin, not in her fur. She would give him whatever he asked if he wished it. But he needed to be responsible for both of them. It was his duty to protect her. And here and now, it was not safe to fuck.

Dammit to hell. He growled at her, causing her to turn and look at him, confusion in her eyes. *Don't tempt me like this, woman.*

She turned on him, snarling in return. *Don't treat me like this.* She didn't understand.

Turning, she took off across the meadow, headed back the way they had come. Leaping after her, he endured the pain of his hardened cock, of the pent-up desire brewing inside him. She would learn that when he said it was okay to fuck, they could fuck, but when he said no, he wouldn't tolerate her snits.

Several deer ran out of the forest, altering their direction quickly when they noticed the two of them, and racing off in the opposite direction. Johann chastised himself immediately for not noticing the change of smells, his thoughts preoccupied with Samantha.

She slowed ahead of him, too, turning to find him behind her, and then sniffing the air.

We're not alone. He caught up with her quickly, nudging into her to keep her going. *Stay next to me,* he growled, unsure what other werewolves were out here.

It didn't take long to reach the truck. He circled it once, insuring their safety, while Samantha changed to her human form and hopped inside. She had her jeans pulled over her hips when he slid in next to her.

"Who else would be running during the daytime?" She asked what he had been wondering.

He didn't like it. If Masterson's pack was that cocky, Bolton would do well to move his pack quickly. They had taken risks running in their fur after the sun was up. But he would never be fool enough to hunt during the daylight.

He dressed quickly, his movements slowed in the limited space, and then headed back toward town. By the time they reached the Inn where he had a room, he knew he needed to tell Bolton about the werewolves hunting. More than likely he would get an earful about taking Samantha out during daylight hours. But he wasn't worried about that. He wanted to know when the pack would be moving, and where Bolton planned on taking them.

But first, he needed to relieve the pent-up energy his little blonde had created.

"I can't believe we didn't notice there were werewolves out there." Samantha stood in front of the mirror on the wall, opposite his bed.

"Which is why we couldn't fuck while we were in our fur." He pulled off his shirt, enjoying how her nipples poked through the fabric of her t-shirt.

She looked at him, realization passing over her pretty face that she'd been the distraction that had prevented him from being more aware.

"I could smell your lust," she said defensively.

"When I say no, it's not because I don't want you." He unbuttoned his jeans and took a step toward her. "I am looking out for us, and you need to trust me."

"I do trust you." She took a step backwards when he approached, reminding him of prey that has just been cornered.

His wild side still lingered in his bloodstream. Grabbing her by the arm, he yanked her to him. She didn't fight when he devoured her mouth, intentionally rough, needing to release the carnal desires he'd denied while in their fur.

Her mouth was hot, her tongue dancing around his while he crushed her to him. Reaching between them, he undid her jeans, tugging at them until they slid past her hips. His cock burned with need, the pressure almost painful. When he felt her fingers brush against his skin while she worked to free him from his jeans, he almost exploded.

He broke the kiss, loving how she gasped for air while hints of silver streaked through her brown eyes. He squatted in front of her, pulling her jeans down and nestling his nose between her legs. "Where do you want me this time?"

"I'm absolutely soaked." She stepped out of her jeans, spreading her legs to allow him to stroke her pussy with his tongue. "Damn, Johann. That feels so good."

"Give me more." He held her hips while stroking her cunt with his tongue. Her thick cream was like nectar, sweet and intoxicating.

He turned her around. "Bend over," he instructed, already painfully hard from just staring at the magnificent view of her shaved pussy and ass.

"Oh, God. Johann." She rested her face on his bed, spreading her arms out as if seeking something to hold on to.

He squeezed and stretched her adorable rear end, running his tongue from one hole to the other.

"I want your ass," he told her, enjoying her groan of approval. Anything. She always gave him anything he wanted, just as eager to experience it as he was.

Blood rushed through him when he stood, his heart throbbing so loudly he could hear it pumping through him. His cock danced an angry and eager dance, as he swore. He needed in her now, or he feared he wouldn't be able to stand much longer, the pressure in his cock at a dangerous level.

"Damn, Samantha." The way she bent over the bed, her expression glazed when she looked over her shoulder at him, brought out all of his animal instincts.

His vision blurred when he slid into her pussy, her gasp of delight enough to put him over the edge. Squeezing her rear he forced himself to stay coherent, to enjoy her moist heat, and not come before he was ready. Her muscles constricted around him, sucking on his cock. Blood surged through him, her heat flushing over him, making him dizzy.

He pulled out of her slowly, her white cream covering his shaft. Dipping in once again, her heat absorbing through him, he barely had the strength to stand.

"Johann." She cried out his name, gripping the blanket with her hands.

"Is this what you wanted?" He barely had the strength to control himself.

"More. I need more." She buried her face in his bed, stifling a cry when he thrust deep inside her.

Moisture soaked his cock, the rich cream seeping around her pussy. Using his thumbs, he traced a pattern with her come from his shaft to her ass.

"I'm going to give you more. Don't worry." His cock hardened even more in anticipation while he soaked the entrance of her rear end with her cream.

"Johann. Oh, God." She lifted her head, turning to look over her shoulder.

The curve of her back, her narrow waist, and wonderfully perfect ass made such an incredible sight. For a moment he moved in and out of her, relishing in how good she felt, and how beautiful she looked.

"I want your ass, baby." He pulled out as he spoke.

"Okay. Yes." Bent over in front of him, her pussy and ass soaked with her white come, she gave herself to him.

He positioned himself, pressing his cockhead against the tight, puckered hole. Pressing gently at first, he immediately felt the tightness of her skin begin to suck him in. So hot. So wet. So willing.

He glided inside her, the tightness of her ass nearly suffocating him. "Dear God." She would squeeze every drop of life right out of him.

"Oh, damn." Her cries fed his carnal nature. She grabbed the bedspread, fisting it in her hands. Arching her back further, she threw her head back, crying out while he drove deep inside her tight ass.

He wanted to pound her ass, ride her without mercy. She was so tight, so incredibly on fire, her heat rode through him like a mad fever.

All he could do was focus on his cock; watch it disappear inside her while he gripped her ass, kneading the soft flesh. She sucked him in, her moisture lubricating his journey, easing his path.

Pressure built, carrying him over. He had to move faster, knowing that doing so would break the dam built up inside him that he could no longer control. Leaning forward, he grabbed the bedspread next to her hands. Lowering himself, he relished in her sweet scent. Her lust was an intoxicating smell while he rode her ass, gliding in and out, faster and faster. The pressure within him rushed through his body, growing painfully. Falling. Floating. She milked him. The dam broke. Pleasure rushed through him until he thought he would pass out.

"Samantha. Dammit." He pulled out just in time to soak her ass with his thick white come, drenching her rear end until he could come no more. "You are incredible, woman," he gasped, collapsing on top of her, then rolling to his side.

She nestled up next to him, her heart pitter-pattering when she pressed her body next to his. "So are you," she whispered, relaxing contentedly in his arms.

Within minutes he knew she was asleep. Kissing her forehead, he lifted her, pulling the blankets down so he could wrap her in them.

"Where are you going?" She stirred, looking up through glazed brown eyes. She had that just fucked and very content look. He loved it.

"I have some things to take care of. Sleep." He kissed her forehead, relishing in her scent one moment longer before he had to leave.

"What do you have to do?" She sounded half awake. So beautiful.

He could so easily blow off his responsibilities and sleep the day away with her.

"I need to talk to Simone." He found his jeans. Already he didn't look forward to the meeting he had to have with the woman who had whelped his cub. But time was running out. The pack would move soon. And he wouldn't lose his daughter.

Samantha stared at him. He knew she didn't understand. She would. He would see to it. But for now, the best thing for her to do was rest. When the pack was ready to move, he would have her by his side. But until then, he had matters to deal with.

Chapter Seven

ഇ

Samantha woke up starving. It was almost dark outside, which meant she'd slept all day. And Johann had been gone all day. After showering, she called Elsa.

"I told Rocky I would spend the night with her, but I guess I'm stranded here."

"I'll be over in a minute." Elsa had told her ten minutes ago. "Rick doesn't want any of the women in the pack going anywhere alone since the Masterson pack seems to be swarming the town."

Now, pacing the small room, she wondered where Johann was. She bounded out the door, ready to get away from that small room, with the rich scent of their lovemaking still lingering in the air. It seemed forever had passed when Elsa finally pulled into the parking lot.

"Did you end up babysitting Jere?" she asked, noticing the cub wasn't with Elsa.

"I watched her for a couple of hours today." Elsa had worn-out jeans on and a snug fitting sweater that showed off her petite figure. She brushed her long blonde hair over her shoulder, smiling at Samantha. "Simone came and got her right before you called. I guess she wasn't too happy with whatever Johann told her. But I'm sure you know all about that."

Samantha didn't have a clue what Johann discussed with Simone. And she was dying to know. She found small satisfaction in the fact that Simone wasn't happy after visiting with him. Now if she could only find out what it was they talked about.

She pondered this while she rode with Elsa. They had pulled into Rick's driveway when Samantha heard gravel crunching behind them. She spotted Rick's truck pulling in behind them when she looked in the rear view mirror.

Both Rick and Johann hopped out of either side of the truck. "Shit," she gasped, as she turned around quickly and looked at her feet. "It's Johann, and I look like shit."

Elsa couldn't stifle a giggle and playfully punched Samantha in the arm. "He's just a werewolf. What impresses me is that the two of them are together — and not fighting."

Elsa's smile disappeared as she turned toward the house. "What the hell?"

Simone sat on the front porch, a suitcase next to her, and Jere on her lap. She stood slowly, tight blue jeans showing off her long thin legs and flat tummy.

The two women got out of the car as the men came up from behind. Rick grabbed Elsa by the back of the neck, kissing her, and then guided her to the house. Johann's attention was on Simone, and Samantha edged near him. She would make sure Simone knew Johann wasn't available.

"I didn't expect such a going-away party." Simone smiled at everyone, but Samantha sensed the tension and fear swarming around the woman.

"What are you talking about, Simone?" Johann sounded dangerous, his tone low and demanding.

Samantha looked from him to Simone, the two of them staring at each other. Simone looked away first, holding her head high, and gripping her daughter's hand. But Johann continued to stare at her, his muscles tense and rippling underneath the shirt he had on.

"I wanted to thank you, Elsa, for letting me into the pack." Simone took a step toward them, but paused, looking at Johann and then quickly back at Elsa. "We're headed back to our home pack. I thought we would say goodbye before we left."

"You would disappear on me again with my cub?" Johann raised his voice, moving in on Simone.

Elsa jumped in between them, but Rick grabbed her, pulling her back to him.

"I didn't disappear on you. You disappeared on me." Simone wrapped her hand around her daughter's head, pressing her to her thigh.

"I didn't know you carried my cub," Johann snarled, then took a step back, running his hand through his hair. "Samantha, take Jere inside. She doesn't need to hear this."

No. She wanted to hear this. Samantha fought the urge to cry out that she didn't want to be left out of this conversation. The sad reality though was none of this was her concern. Johann had a past, and he was right. If voices were raised, the cub didn't need to be part of it.

"It's okay, sweetheart. Samantha is a wonderful lady. I'll be inside in just a minute," she heard Simone whisper to her daughter.

Samantha took the little cub's hand and went inside. She was glad when she found a TV show that Jere liked. Samantha relaxed, admitting she'd been worried the cub wouldn't want to be with her, but with Simone.

"I'll see if I can find you some juice, sweetheart." She ran her hand over the cub's pale blond hair, noticing again that she had her father's eyes.

She walked into the kitchen and put her fists on the counter, taking short, quick breaths, trying to calm the carnal instincts that made her so much more than human. Her blood begged to pump faster. Her bones ached to grow. Her muscles hurt with the desire to give her strength...strength to kill with her bare hands. She couldn't remember the last time fury overpowered her ability to control when she changed into fur.

And she was just as angry with Johann as she was with herself. He had pushed her away, leaving without discussing what he planned to do earlier. It was as if his private affairs were none of her concern. Well, she wasn't a doormat, to be used and cast aside when matters of importance came up.

She forced her hands to relax on the counter and noted the silence outside. Where was Johann? Had he left with Simone? It didn't sound like he would have been willing to drive her to the bus station. And Simone didn't sound like she would leave without her daughter. She closed her eyes and prayed for patience when she heard footsteps approaching. She gathered all the strength she could and turned around, hoping she appeared composed.

"Thank you for bringing her inside." Simone held Jere in her arms, and stopped in the doorway to the kitchen. Her eyes drifted around the room. "This is a nice house."

Since Samantha had little to do with how nice the house was, she simply nodded her head. She relaxed her facial muscles when she focused on Jere.

"How old is she?" Samantha tried to get the little cub to smile.

"Three." Simone gave her daughter a slight squeeze.

Elsa appeared behind her, smiling at the cub. "We can put you in a room upstairs. Although to be honest, I don't know how long we'll be here. Rick is talking about moving us soon."

Samantha felt her gut tighten into a knot. She strolled toward the front door, pausing when she noticed Rick and Johann out front in what appeared to be a rather heated discussion. Once again she wondered if Johann would move with the pack. The only thing she knew for sure at this point was that he didn't want Simone and Jere going anywhere without him.

Taking a deep breath, she pushed open the screen door, and stepped out on to the porch.

"Johann. You need a committee formed to take a cub from its mother. There's pack law to consider." Rick stopped talking when he saw her and ran his hand through his tousled hair.

"I don't plan on breaking any laws." Johann noticed her and moved to her quickly, grabbing her hand.

She barely had time to think before he dragged her past Rick. "Walk with me. I need the fresh air."

"Are you going to tell me what is going on?" she asked after she'd managed to keep up with his stride for over a block.

"I want my daughter with me." He didn't add any more information. Apparently he felt that summed it up.

She nodded, seeing the determined set of his jaw. Cool air wrapped around her, the smells of the city drowning out the fragrance the breeze brought. Her thoughts were in turmoil though, and she needed some answers. She had to have some kind of direction, anything just so she could have peace of mind.

"Do you plan on moving with the pack?" she asked, looking up at him, searching his expression.

"I think it's the best idea for the time being," he told her, taking her hand when they crossed the street.

Her mind raced. Johann had no idea how worried she was about being with him. Therefore it wasn't something he was concerned about. Either he assumed they would stay together when the pack moved, or their being together wasn't foremost on his mind.

"I guess I should start packing." Her small apartment wouldn't take long to organize.

"You're right." He looked at her as if that thought hadn't crossed his mind. "Pack only what you absolutely need to have, and we'll haul everything else to Goodwill."

Once again Johann left her, this time at her apartment. "I'll call you later tonight," he told her after kissing her on the forehead. "Maybe you can talk Rocky into helping you get stuff sorted."

It was a good idea. Rocky's place would need to be cleaned out too.

"The big chore will be packing Rick's home," Rocky told her later that evening after they'd managed to pack up her tiny apartment. "My place won't take much longer than it did here."

It was after midnight when they finally had both places cleaned and organized. Rocky sat down in the middle of her living room when the phone rang.

"Do you want to run with Rick, Elsa and Marty?" she asked, her smile showing she liked the idea.

"I think I'd rather take a shower." And figure out where in the hell Johann had disappeared too. At least she knew Simone was staying next door, and so he wasn't with her.

Someone rapped on the front door, and she knew her delight was obvious when she grinned from ear to ear at the sight of Johann.

"You two could earn a living doing this," he teased, glancing around at stacked boxes and trash bags.

"Not on your life," Rocky retorted, pushing herself to her feet. "Well, I'm going to go run with the others. You two have a good night."

The others stood outside waiting. Samantha barely had the energy to tell them good night before she climbed into Johann's truck.

Later that night, she stretched contentedly under the warm blankets. Johann's long body kept her entire side warm. She reveled in how well their bodies fit together. The cool air in Johann's room tickled her nose. Hints of moonlight peeking through the closed curtains, begged her to come out and play. Silently, she slid out from under the covers and padded across the cold floor.

"I'm going to follow you." A rumbly voice spoke from underneath the blankets.

Samantha giggled, thrilled at the idea. "Hmm, should I let him catch me, or not?" she mumbled loud enough for him to hear.

She slid into her jeans, then grabbed her sweatshirt and ran from the room, without putting it on, when Johann growled again and worked to untangle the covers.

Fall would come early this year—and it would be a short season. The night air slapped at her cheeks the second she shut the motel room door behind her. It was a shame she couldn't run alone. But she knew she had to wait for Johann to appear, and then walk through town with him before allowing the change.

The cold night air woke her up. Even though she knew they had only slept a few hours, she was glad they weren't missing at least some of the evening. Johann held her close while they walked, until they reached the edge of town, where the trees grew thicker. They were trudging through the forest when Johann decided it was okay to strip out of their clothes.

The change rippled through her, and she danced under the moonlight as she trotted through the trees. Breaking into a full-fledged run, she left Johann behind. Dried leaves crunched behind her, and she knew Johann was in hot pursuit.

The cold air made her frisky, and she darted to the side, willing to play a game of cat and mouse. But as she curved to the right, Johann barreled into her, and she rolled over crushed leaves, the world spinning around her.

What the hell? It took her a minute to realize that his instinct worked in full beast mode. He would take what he wanted.

She struggled to get to her feet, but a powerful werewolf hovered over her, his glossy white fur filling her vision. His cock was huge, protruding between his hind legs, and he growled and nipped at her ear, sending sweet pain rushing through her.

You will submit, my sweet bitch, his growl seemed to say. She had never considered saying no. Besides, he had her trapped.

And she didn't want to deny him. *I am your sweet little bitch.* She growled and looked up into possessive eyes, his massive head hovering over hers, lust clouding his expression, dagger-like teeth pointing down at her.

He pressed his cock against her leg, and she lifted her tail to the side, allowing him access. She watched his eyes cloud over, and he didn't hesitate in driving into her.

Holy shit! She yelped at the new sensation, his long thick cock, shaped differently than in his human form, plowing into the narrow crevice of her werewolf pussy.

She laid on her side, and spread her hind legs so that he could penetrate her further, slide deeper into her hot cunt, fill her with his animal cock.

His hindquarters begin to move, as he speared her again and again, building pressure unlike any she had ever experienced as a woman.

This carnal act was raw, untamed, and without pretense. Instinct drove her, her body filling with an orgasm, thicker and hotter than any she had felt up until now. He showed no mercy, beating her with his cock, slamming her tender pussy, filling her womb with a pressure that only he could appease.

She cried out, howling underneath him, which seemed to feed his madness and make him beat her soul with his lust. He grew inside her, with each plunge he swelled, her pussy juices soaking both of them, until he impaled her with so much force she thought she would slide out from underneath him. But his cock held her in place, gripping her from within, securing her, locking the two of them, bonding them together.

She panted underneath him, sated and content, feeling the security of her world around him as he hovered over her. Minutes passed, the world around them calm in respect, until finally he slid out of her. He nudged her swollen pussy with his nose, and she spread her legs willingly as he stroked her fiery hole with his tongue.

You are so good, she wanted to cry out, his tongue sending her into a state of bliss. But her beast's mouth could only growl her pleasure. He speared her tender pussy with the tip of his tongue, lapping up their cum, and she felt her insides swell once again.

Shit. Oh, shit. She yelped and contorted her body, but his large head between her hind legs made it too hard to move. Wave after wave of sweet pleasure rippled through her, like a fresh spring racing over jagged rocks. She exploded, gushing with hot cum, filling the air with her beast's lust.

When she opened her eyes, Johann stood, looking down at her, his long red tongue licking her cum from the fur on his face. He looked very, very pleased with himself.

She struggled to stand, proving that four wobbly legs were no better than two, and he gently gripped the nape of her neck with his teeth until she had the strength to move.

They loped side-by-side back to where their clothes were, and she dressed quickly after changing into her human form. Turning she saw Johann watched her in his fur.

Slowly, he walked toward her. With him in his animal form, they were almost eye-to-eye. He was a huge, menacing looking creature. Samantha held her hand out and rubbed the side of his head. He pushed his head into her hand. She could feel teeth as long as her palm, brush across her skin.

He continued to move closer until he rested his head on her shoulder and tickled the nape of her neck with his cold nose. She wrapped her arms around his huge neck, and he was almost able to lift her feet from the ground.

"I love you." She kissed the coarse white hair on his cheek, and he blinked at her, then took his huge red tongue and licked her across her face.

"Johann!" she cried out, and then rolled over realizing she wiped her face with the blanket, and not her sweater.

It had been a dream. Nothing but a dream. She looked up into his sleeping face, wondering if she'd actually spoken out loud. And if so, had she just told him she loved him?

Chapter Eight

ॐ

Over the next couple of days, the pack seemed to be in complete disarray. Rick held several meetings, and Samantha heard along with the others that the house Elsa had bought would be their new home.

"It used to be an old boarding house." Elsa glowed with excitement when she described the place to them. "I know it needs a little work, but we can make it our home, and it sits on a thousand acres. All of that will be pack land. We can build on it, hunt on it, live the way we are supposed to live."

A few members approached Rick telling him they were moving on to another pack, but most agreed to go. Now the men went from home to home, helping to pack, load furniture, and haul unnecessary items to charity centers.

She stood in the kitchen that morning at Elsa and Rick's house, talking to Rocky, while they pulled pictures from the walls, cleaning and packing at the same time. Simone had left early that morning, leaving Jere with them. The cub sat on the floor playing with several dolls Johann had bought her.

Elsa stacked another picture on the table when the phone rang.

"What is it?" Samantha noticed Elsa's worried look after she hung up the phone.

"Miranda is down at the diner." Elsa chewed her lip while she looked down at Jere. Rocky had sat on the floor, looking much like a little girl herself, helping to dress the dolls. "We better head down there."

She left the kitchen, Samantha and Rocky right behind her.

"Simone just left with a couple of Masterson's pack members," she whispered, keeping her eye on the kitchen. Obviously she didn't want Jere to hear. "But she didn't look to happy to be leaving with them. Miranda is worried that she is in trouble."

Damn. Damn. Damn.

"Someone needs to stay with Jere." Rocky glanced back toward the kitchen, the cub now singing to herself in the other room.

"I don't want to go alone." Elsa looked at both of them.

"I'll go with you." Samantha knew she had more street sense than Elsa or Rocky, but she never dreamed she would use it to rescue Simone.

"We need to find the men," Elsa said after backing her car out of the drive. "I know they planned on packing up several dens this morning."

"Did Miranda have any idea where Simone and the werewolves were headed?" Samantha stared out the window, trying to figure out why Simone would agree to go with the other pack members if she didn't want to.

"One of the werewolves had mentioned killing some time playing pool. I guess they would have gone to the bar."

"Why don't you drop me off there? Wait long enough for me to find out if she is there. And then you can go find the men," Samantha suggested.

"I can't leave you alone like that." Elsa shook her head. "Rick would have my neck. Not to mention Johann would be outraged if I left you in a situation like that."

Samantha looked down at what she was wearing. Loose fitting jeans and a sweatshirt, and she wasn't wearing makeup. "Look," she said. "There is a reason why Simone left with them. And I doubt it was to partake in an orgy."

Elsa looked at her wide-eyed, but quickly turned her attention to the road.

"All I need to do is find out why she is with them. No one will notice me." She gestured at her attire, knowing she was far from attractive at the moment. "Believe me. If they have Simone, they won't give me a second glance."

"Don't cut yourself short." Elsa frowned, but turned in the direction of the bar. "You are a lot prettier than Simone."

Elsa must not see Simone for the sexy woman that she was. More than likely because they had grown up together. But Samantha smiled at the compliment anyway.

Elsa pulled into the parking lot, and the two of them stared at the bar for a moment. Not many cars were there this early in the day. And those that were parked in the gravel lot looked familiar.

"I'll let you know if they are in there." Samantha jumped out, her stomach in knots. She had no idea how she would play this out if Simone were in the bar.

Her eyes adjusted quickly to the softly lit pool hall while she stood in the doorway for a minute. Simone sat at the other end on a bar stool, her back to the door, watching a couple of men play pool. Samantha noticed immediately the black mini-skirt Simone wore with black pantyhose and flat black boots. Even with the baggy sweater she had on, Simone turned heads. She was no comparison to the sexy, well-built bitch.

Turning and nodding to Elsa, she entered the bar, wondering if she even had any cash on her. Maybe she hadn't planned this out so well. And Simone didn't appear to be in any real danger.

One of the men playing pool must have made a good shot. He whooped with delight, turning to Simone and pulling her off the bar stool. The werewolf kissed her soundly, running his hand up underneath her mini-skirt. Simone didn't appear to be resisting, but she almost fell onto her bar stool when he let her go. The other werewolf laughed, and then he came up to Simone, grabbing her by the hair, and leaning her head back while he stuck his tongue down her throat.

Samantha thought she might gag. Her mouth went dry, and she leaned against the bar counter, trying to figure out what to do.

"What can I get you?" The bartender glanced her way, but then looked to the end of the bar where Simone sat.

"Give us another round," the werewolf who had just made the good shot yelled. He was a heavyset man with bushy brown hair. Simone could do a lot better. "And get the pretty lady down there her drink too."

Simone did turn around then and stared at her. A nasty green bruise covered her cheek. Samantha simply stared for a moment, realizing they had already roughed her up a bit.

Simone stood and walked toward her. "Get out of here. Now." She didn't smile, and her words were harsh.

"Not without you." Samantha straightened, not breaking eye contact with the pretty *Lunewulf* bitch.

"I can't leave. But you can. Go get help if you want. But get the hell out of here." There was a desperate edge to Simone's tone.

"Help is on its way." Or at least she hoped so. She lowered her voice, noticing one of the werewolves had realized Simone no longer sat with them. "Let's go. You know we can outrun them."

The heavyset werewolf started toward them, a leer on his face. "You got a friend, little bitch?" he asked.

Light flooded the bar when the door opened behind Samantha. Simone's eyes grew wide at the same time Samantha smelled outrage. It saturated the air around her. She didn't have time to turn around before large hands grabbed her, causing her to stumble backwards.

"Get out to the car. Now!" Johann sounded more furious than she'd ever heard him sound.

"You don't have to talk to her like that." Simone jumped to her defense, surprising her.

Samantha regained her footing, turning to look at Simone. But Rick and Marty were right behind Johann, and they all moved in front of her. She barely saw Johann grab Simone, lifting her from the ground. He turned to glare at her.

"Go to the car, Samantha. Move it."

She turned and hurried out of the bar, her entire body shaking.

"Are you okay?" Elsa asked, pushing the passenger door open for her. Rick's truck idled next to Elsa's car, and from how it was parked, it looked like the werewolves had skid to a stop right in front of the bar. "Where is Simone?"

"I'm fine."

She didn't have to say anymore. The two of them watched the werewolves leave the bar with Simone among them. Simone said something to Rick, and then fell backwards into Johann when Rick looked like he would strangle her. Simone obviously said something disrespectful, because Rick looked like he would wring her neck. He left her clinging to Johann and strolled over to Elsa's car. She rolled her window down partially. Johann opened the back door and almost shoved Simone inside.

"We'll meet you back at the house." Rick tapped the top of Elsa's car with his hand and then turned toward his truck.

"Are you okay?" Samantha got a closer look at Simone's bruised face. Werewolves healed quickly. The bruise would be gone by the next day.

"I'm fine." She didn't look fine. "I'm sure those brutes will believe what they want, but if I hadn't gone with them, Bolton and his cronies were headed over to your house, Elsa. They knew Rick wasn't there."

"Oh, shit." Elsa twisted to look at Simone. "Did you tell Rick that?"

"Not yet." Simone shrugged, looking past them out the front windshield.

The three men had climbed into the truck. Rick honked for Elsa to get moving. Samantha straightened in her seat. Worry made the inside of the car stink.

The werewolves who had been in the bar walked into the parking lot, glaring at Rick's truck.

"Your pack won't live through the night, Bolton."

Samantha clasped her hands in her lap to keep them from shaking.

Chapter Nine

ઝ

Simone stared at them defiantly, daring them to challenge anything she said. She hadn't changed a bit over the years.

"I don't think you understand." Johann ran his hands through his hair, walking over to stare out the front window. "You can't act like this anymore. You have a cub. Responsibilities."

"You can't take her away from me." Simone glanced at Rick, who leaned in the doorway toward the kitchen, listening.

Johann didn't need to look at the pack leader. "Prove yourself unfit, and you're damned straight I can take her."

She grabbed his arm, her thin fingers cold against his skin. "Do you hate me that much, Johann?" Her expression contorted with grief, the scent of it almost drowning out her musky perfume. "I am a good mother. Jere was kept safe. She was never exposed to any danger. I did what I did for the pack, for Elsa...for Samantha."

He studied her, those blue eyes as light as a summer sky but with too much eye makeup. Her lips had a natural rose color, and her blonde hair had streaks of highlights he was sure she paid good money to have done every month. She looked a lot older than she used to.

She sighed, looking away from him. "I'm sorry that I scared Elsa and the other bitches," she told Rick.

He nodded, turning when the phone rang. She glanced back at Johann, her gaze lowering, taking in his physique. When she looked him in the eye again, her defiance had returned. Tossing her hair over her shoulder she left the room.

Rick returned from the kitchen, holding the cordless phone in his hand. "Tonight I will turn this territory over to Masterson. We leave in the morning."

The decision to turn good hunting land over to the other pack had been a tough one. Johann saw the turmoil rage in Bolton's eyes, but he admired the werewolf for possessing the strength to make the right decision for his pack.

"You and Samantha can stay here tonight, if you wish."

"Sounds good." Johann glanced up the stairs, knowing the women bonded while they comforted Simone. Maybe it would allow Samantha and Simone the opportunity to become friends. He hoped so.

Later that night he woke to Samantha's dreaming again. Her murmuring stirred him and he pulled her closer where they slept together on the living room floor. Pulling the covers over them, he ran his hand over her soft skin, relishing in the soft contours of her body.

Her chest rose and fell with her quick breathing. Johann cupped her breast, her nipple puckering against his skin. She mumbled something, her voice a mere whisper, teasing his senses, like a soft breeze on a warm day. Turning, she cuddled into him, nestling her body against his. He was hard in an instant, throbbing, aching to be inside her. The heat between her legs called to him, her moist heat spreading over him, burning through to his very soul.

"Johann." She spoke his name on a breath.

He forgot to breathe, dared not move, but cradled her, waiting to hear the words. She had told him she loved him before in her sleep. And although she had been dreaming, her feelings had come forth and expressed what she wasn't able to tell him when she was awake. He waited, hoping to hear her say them again.

But her breathing slowed, her body relaxing against his. The softness of her skin soothed him, and he knew he would have to accept that. His precious Samantha slipped into a deeper sleep, her dream having ended.

Johann didn't remember falling asleep, but when he woke up, Samantha wasn't by his side. Moving quickly, he grabbed his clothes, noting it was barely light outside. Relief overwhelmed him when he found her in the kitchen, her hair tousled and sleep still making her soft brown eyes look glazed.

"Want some coffee?" she asked him. "Rick and Marty are already outside loading the vehicles."

Within an hour they were on the road, headed for Canada and their new home. Johann saw immediately why Elsa fell in love with the old place when they pulled up. They were out in the middle of nowhere, open land spreading around them for miles.

The place needed a lot of work. But voices of approval sang out while they trudged through the place, hauling in furniture and unloading boxes.

"Where are you going?" Johann paused on the wide staircase when Samantha started down the hallway on the second floor.

"This is where my room is going to be." She held a box of her things in her arms, a smudge of dirt streaked across her face. She blew at a strand of hair. "Elsa assigned all of our rooms to us right after we got here. Simone and Jere have that room." She nodded her head to the closed door nearest her. "I have this next room. Elsa and Rick are on the other side of me, and Rocky is at the end of the hall."

Mighty convenient how Rick had his single bitches within earshot. He adjusted the box in his arms. "Well, let's see if your room is any bigger than mine."

He followed the soft sway of her ass down the hall, enjoying how her faded blue jeans hugged her just right. More than anything he wanted to slide his hand along the seat of her pants, feel her heat through the material, hear her moan from his touch.

"The rooms on the third floor are a lot smaller." He put his box down on a chair by the door, and took in the solid woodwork that was in every room.

One large window offered plenty of light, enough to see that re-varnishing the floor and baseboards would be enough to make this room sparkle. Everything seemed to be solid.

"We have to share a bathroom that is at the end of the hall, but otherwise, it's really nice." She dropped her box on the floor, the thud echoing in the empty room.

"It's the same way on the third floor." He turned at the sounds of footsteps on the stairs. Marty and Rocky talked to each other as they started down the hall. "Marty, Toby and I will be sharing a bathroom."

He closed the bedroom door, noticing it didn't lock.

"What are you doing?" Samantha asked, her voice much quieter than a second before.

"I'm going to fuck you."

She smiled instantly, her nipples puckering eagerly through her shirt. But then she crossed her arms over her chest, glancing past him, hearing the commotion going on just outside their room.

"What if someone comes in here?"

"Then they will see me making love to you."

"What if it's Jere?" Excitement radiated around her, making her smell even sweeter than usual.

He wouldn't give up this moment. There was a lot of work to do, and he knew they would be busy for the rest of the day arranging furniture in all of the rooms. Turning, he slid the chair with the box on it in front of the door.

"Come here." He told her, loving the glow that flushed her cheeks.

She didn't hesitate, walking into his arms and pressing her soft body against his.

"We don't have much time," he told her, wishing he could enjoy every inch of her.

"I know." She gasped when he tugged at her jeans, freeing the buttons with one hand.

She helped him ease the material past her hips, her rich creamy smell filling the air around them instantly. Her scent intoxicated him, filling his senses like a wildfire. An aching pressure surged through him, gripping him like an untamed beast. He craved her like no other woman. Just touching her, feeling her soft skin under his fingertips, made him crazy with need.

"I need to fuck you now." He grasped at his buttons on his jeans, tearing at them eagerly. His cock needed freedom before the pain made him explode. How she managed to make him harder than steel just by being around her, he had no clue.

"Yes, Johann." She ran her hands under his shirt, her small hands grazing over his chest. Her touch was like a wave of electricity, charging his muscles, making them itch to grow.

She brought out the beast in him; carnal and wild, he could barely think when she wrapped her arms around him. Her soft lips brushed against his, moist and hot. He needed more, had to be inside her in every way possible.

Spearing her mouth with his tongue, he swallowed her gasp, lifted her while he devoured her mouth. Her hands were in his hair, brushing over his cheeks, touching him everywhere, charging him with a need he couldn't master.

He barely had his cock free, his pants hugging his hips, the material parted enough so that his hardness was no longer confined. And when she wrapped her thin legs around him, clinging to him, her heat absorbed through his shaft, saturated his scrotum, drowning him before he was even inside her.

"Damn, woman." He pressed her back against the wall, catching his breath while he reached between them, positioning his cock at her entrance.

She thrust her pussy forward. "Now, Johann. Fuck me now."

He dove deep inside her, her muscles parting and sucking him in. It took all his strength to hold her up, her heat sweltering, burning him while he buried himself deep inside her.

When she would have cried out, he pressed his mouth to hers, allowing her to release her passion into his mouth. Her tongue danced with his while he impaled her again. Her muted gasp was buried in their kiss, hot and passionate. She dug her nails into his shoulders, her thighs clamped against his hips while he fucked her, pounded her hot cunt while her thick juices threatened to drown him.

The room filled with the scent of their lust, hot and heady, so thick he could hardly breathe. With every thrust, his cock grew, pressure building so fast he couldn't control it.

"I'm going to come," he hissed, breathing heavily into her mouth.

"Yes," she cried, her muscles tightening around him, suffocating him while her orgasm ripped through her.

She held him so tightly while her body shook, her heat absorbed through him, filling him with power like no one else could give him. The dam broke inside him, his juices streaming through him like hot lava. He fought to catch his breath while he emptied himself deep inside her.

A solid knock on the door made Samantha jump. She clung to him, gasping.

"Some of us have work to do," Marty teased, his laughter echoing in the hallway.

Rocky giggled, their footsteps fading as they reached the stairwell.

Chapter Ten

ॐ

There were only a few packs in Ontario. Over the following weeks, each pack leader welcomed them to the district. Elsa and Johann served as interpreters to the French pack leader who visited from a territory north of them.

"There are no packs within several hundred miles of us," Rick told all of them while they sat around the long dining room table. "You couldn't have purchased a more prime piece of land if you'd spent months researching the project."

He beamed at Elsa, who blushed beautifully.

"But you bought it on a whim," Rick added. "And that reinforces my belief that we are destined to be successful in our new territory."

"Here. Here." Marty raised his water glass, offering a toast.

Samantha lifted her glass, too, along with the others. The smell of the steaks lingered in the air, and the rich irony aroma of the greens distracted her. Maybe the huge meal after helping wallpaper the living room all day had been too much.

"I'm not clearing your dishes for you," Miranda announced. "If anyone wants some of my chocolate cake, you better get your dishes in the sink and scraped."

A loud scuffling of chairs sounded, everyone talking at once.

"Cake." Jere cried out her excitement. "Mommy, I want some cake."

"You're on kitchen duty with me." Rocky nudged Samantha, pointing at the schedule Elsa had printed up and hung on the refrigerator.

"We'll eat our cake later." Rick already headed toward the back door. "Werewolves, let's get back to work."

Samantha glanced out the back door at the house frame that stood behind one of the outbuildings. Marty had announced to everyone that he had finally gotten Rick to approve of him mating with Rocky. Ever since then the men had been working on a cottage out back for the two of them. Johann swatted her on the rear end before following the others out back.

She envied Rocky, but kept her feelings to herself. She had no idea how Johann felt about her, other than the fact that he loved to fuck her.

You're being too hard on the werewolf. She knew her emotions were running high right now. Johann cared for her very much. She saw that in his actions. And as isolated as they were, she knew he wasn't seeing any other bitches.

"I can't believe how quickly everyone has bonded." Elsa stared out the back door, watching the men get to work.

"Isn't it wonderful?" Rocky started giggling. "And I wish you all would have told me how wonderful sex was a long time ago."

Elsa burst out laughing, turning and wrapping her arms around her friend. "Rick would have killed me if I'd done that."

"Rocky, you've gone and fallen in love." Simone chuckled, her deep sultry laugh causing her daughter to giggle too.

"It's wonderful." Rocky rinsed the dishes she'd been scrubbing and put them in the strainer. "I swear he tells me he loves me every five minutes."

Samantha forced a smile. Johann may not love her, but he did care about her. She would have to accept that. She scraped the leftovers into dishes to save as late night snacks after their runs. Hopefully the men wouldn't work too late into the evening. A late-night run with wild sex under the country sky sounded like a perfect end to the day.

Ever since they'd started working on the cottage out back, Johann hadn't come to her room as much. Often he would stop by to kiss her good night, and then tell her he needed to get some sleep. Only once had he snuck her upstairs to sleep with him. She sighed, craving his warm touch, those powerful arms wrapped around her. Life just seemed better when she was with him.

"As soon as we're through here, I'll help you sort through that video collection you've got." Rocky looked at her, her tone softer.

Samantha wondered if her emotions could be smelled. "That would be great." She didn't feel like spending the evening alone in her bedroom anyway.

"Look what I've got." Simone sauntered into Samantha's bedroom that evening after having put Jere to bed.

Rocky and Elsa sat on the floor, looking through the boxes of videos while Samantha stood at her shelves. All three women looked up at Simone.

"Wine," Elsa explained, grinning at the bottle in Simone's hand. "I'll go get some cups."

"No need." She extended her teeth and pulled the cork out of the bottle. "We don't want to draw attention to ourselves by going downstairs."

She offered the open bottle to Elsa, respecting her title as queen bitch.

"This will be fun." Elsa held the bottle in her hands, turning it, watching the fluid inside. "The men all went on a run, claiming the territory as theirs. And with Miranda and the others asleep, we can have our own little party."

Elsa sipped and then offered the bottle to Samantha. She stared at the blood-colored fluid inside.

"We can get drunk and share all of our dark secrets," Simone said.

Samantha looked up at her, wondering what dark secrets she had. Glancing back at the bottle, she took a small sip. It tasted nothing like blood but went down almost as easily. Her stomach bubbled around the intrusion. She passed the bottle to Rocky.

"I don't know if I should." Rocky stared at the bottle.

"Why not?" Elsa asked.

Instead of taking the bottle, Rocky looked down at her hands, her soft brown curls falling around her face. When she looked up, tears had welled in her eyes. One streamed a path down her cheek.

"Ohh..." Simone rubbed her hands together. "You've got a secret to share."

"What's wrong?" Elsa scooted over to Rocky, wrapping her arm around her shoulder.

Samantha's gut clenched, guessing Rocky's secret before she shared it. Simone's perfume dominated over the other scents in the room, but she thought she detected a more earthy aroma around Rocky.

"My guess is you're pregnant." Simone still smiled. "Your emotions will go crazy for a while. But don't worry, honey. A little wine won't hurt anything."

"You don't get it." Rocky looked up, snapping at Simone. "Marty has all of these plans. Our house won't be done until the spring. And he and Rick have discussed so many other projects they want to do with this land. All of it will take money. They will both kill me if they find out I'm pregnant."

"You're wrong, Rocky." Elsa soothed her friend, stroking the curls from her face. "Those two will be more excited than cubs to learn that our pack is growing. We will be on this land for the rest of our lives. They will always have projects lined up."

Rocky looked up with a glimmer of hope.

"So you haven't told anyone?" Samantha asked.

"No one. Well, not until now." Rocky looked at her, smiling through her tears.

"Well, congratulations!" Simone raised her bottle in the air. "And at least you know that your werewolf will be happy with the news when you tell him he will have a cub."

Samantha stiffened. She knew Simone implied Johann wouldn't have wanted to know he was going to be a father.

"You're not being fair," Elsa scolded Simone. Obviously she caught the implication, too. "You never even told Johann he was going to have a cub."

Simone sighed, plopping down on the bed and running her hand down the back of Samantha's hair.

"You're right." She took another sip of the wine, then handed it to Samantha. "But it wasn't the same. Johann and I were never in love. We both ran wild with our pack. You remember, don't you, Elsa?"

Samantha didn't take a sip, but watched over the bottle as Elsa nodded.

"I always envied you for being able to do what you wanted." Elsa made a face. "Grandmother always kept me under lock and key."

"There were days when I wished someone would have kept a closer eye on me." Simone sighed. "But that was a wild time. We were all young. And I admit that I ran with more than one werewolf. I knew the cub was Johann's, but worried that he wouldn't believe me. So I left the pack."

"Why did you seek him out, then?" Samantha knew her voice sounded cold. She glanced at Simone, who seemed to watch her carefully. She looked down at her hands, aching to hear the answer, but not sure she wanted to know the truth.

"Time had passed." Simone sounded gentle.

She didn't want to hurt her. Samantha sensed that.

"Jere had a right to know her father, and Johann had a right to know he'd sired a cub." Simone stood up, walking around the women on the floor and staring out the window into the darkness. "I didn't realize Johann would be so possessive though."

"What do you mean?" Samantha stared at Simone's back, hoping Johann didn't plan to make Simone his mate out of duty. Her heart clenched at the thought. She stared at Simone's highlighted hair that fell over her shoulder blades, her narrow waist accented by her snug jeans. What werewolf wouldn't want her?

Simone turned around. "He won't let go of Jere. I can go where I want, but he will keep Jere if I leave." She shrugged, looking sincerely sorry. "I guess you are stuck with me."

A wave of relief flushed through Samantha. But she glanced at the other women around sitting around her. "Johann can't forcibly take Jere from you, can he?"

"Pack law can be grossly antiquated." Elsa made a face.

"She's right," Simone nodded her head at Elsa. "My past is spotted, to say the least. I was a slut." She raised her arms in an exaggerated shrug. "Just ask anyone from my old pack. If Johann wanted to use that against me to take Jere, he could find grounds to do it."

"I don't think Johann would do that. You're a good mommy." And Samantha meant it. She'd never known Johann to be as coldhearted as Simone suggested.

"I'm glad you feel that way." Simone moved across the room again, sitting down carefully on the edge of Samantha's bed. "I have a feeling you and I will be spending a lot of time together in the future. Johann isn't going to let either one of us go."

Chapter Eleven

ഇ

Samantha rolled over in her bed later that night, muted voices coming from downstairs tickling her ears. By the time she reached the bottom of the stairs, the hushed voices had her attention.

She strolled into the living room, noticing the empty bottle of wine on the coffee table. Simone lay sprawled out on the couch, her shirt untucked and her feet bare. Johann sat at the end of the couch, looking distracted but not drunk like Simone. Elsa sat across from them, her knees pulled up to her chest.

"What's going on here?" she asked, glancing from one of them to the other.

"Ding dong. The witch is dead." Simone sang the familiar tune while wagging her finger in the air.

"Don't be so disrespectful." Johann slapped Simone's leg, and then stood to face Samantha.

"Ouch," Simone cried out in an exaggerated tone. "Don't play the righteous one, Johann. No one liked her. And you know it."

Johann ignored her. "I got a call a couple of hours ago," he told Samantha. "Grandmother Rousseau had a heart attack. She's dead."

Samantha nodded, noting he didn't smell sad. She glanced passed him at Elsa. She had rested her head on her knees, staring blankly.

"I'm sorry to hear that," she said.

Elsa looked up at her, her expression serious. "We must look like an odd lot of mourners. But you have to understand.

We all ran from her, but she raised us. She gave my sisters and me a home after our parents died. She helped Simone with her schooling. And she was our pack leader all of our lives."

"And now she needs a proper funeral ceremony." Johann turned from her, heading toward the kitchen. "I need to get some sleep." He touched her cheek, his rough fingers sending a tingling through her body. "We'll discuss this more in the morning."

Samantha watched him head toward the stairs.

"He's leaving, you know." Simone's comment caught her attention.

"What?" Samantha felt her gut clench. "What do you mean?"

"Simone. You're out of line." Elsa stood also, stretching.

"You know he is in line to be pack leader. Do you think he will pass up that opportunity?" Simone picked up the empty bottle of wine, realized it was empty, and put it back down. "He is going to go take on our old pack. And he will take Jere with him."

"Is that what he said?" Samantha turned to look at the empty staircase again, suddenly having the urge to hurry up to his room and demand the truth.

"No. He didn't say that." Elsa hurried to reassure her.

"He said they want him to return and be the new pack leader." Simone stretched out on the couch. "He won't say no."

Samantha had heard enough. If Johann was leaving, she needed to know now. She turned and headed toward the stairs.

"Samantha, wait." Elsa was queen bitch, and Samantha honored the title.

But she couldn't wait. She turned, facing Elsa in the dark kitchen when her friend approached her. "I've waited long enough, Elsa," she said quietly. "He takes me as a mate now. Or he never will."

Elsa stared at her for a moment and then simply nodded. "Be quiet about it. You know Rick's rules about bitches being on the third floor."

Yes, she knew. Rick could be way too old-fashioned sometimes.

She pattered up the stairs, stepping gingerly to avoid stepping on any loose floorboards. She was grateful when she started ascending to the third floor that Elsa stomped up to the second floor. Hopefully, if Samantha made any noise it wouldn't be heard over Elsa.

It was warm in the hallway, and sweat prickled on her skin between her breasts. She paused in front of Johann's door, sucking in air, building the confidence needed to confront him. Raising her fist to knock, she paused, deciding that might make too much noise. Werewolves could have annoyingly sensitive hearing in their sleep.

Her hand was sweaty when she grabbed the doorknob. She turned it before she lost her nerve.

Johann lay in his bed, the covers over him to his waist. His hands were clasped behind his head, and he appeared to have been staring at the ceiling. His expression didn't change when she entered his room and closed the door quietly behind her.

"We need to talk." She felt her heart skip a beat, his predatory eyes devouring her. Licking her lips, she approached his bed, and went to kneel on it.

"No." His word made her freeze.

Her heart swelled to an unpleasant lump in her throat. Was he turning her away?

"You don't climb into bed with me with your clothes on."

Relief washed over her. She stripped out of her clothes, dropping them on the floor while he watched her.

Once again she knelt on the bed, noticing the covers move as his dick hardened. She wanted to wipe her palms on the comforter, force herself to be calm enough not to sweat. How enticing. Here she knelt before him, sweating like a pig.

"Why are you nervous?" He hadn't moved, his hands still clasped behind his head, his blue eyes smoldering like a thunderhead ready to explode.

Her mouth was suddenly too dry to speak. Reaching for the covers, she pulled them down so she could see his cock, so hard, so thick and ready for her. She ran her fingers over the swollen roundness of his cockhead. His stomach muscles tightened, while muscles constricted in his chest. She stroked her fingers down his shaft, feeling his power, feeding off of his strength.

"Are you leaving this pack?" she managed to ask.

She moved closer, his heady sexual scent drawing her to him. Leaning forward, pressing her breasts against her knees, she rubbed her nose against his cock, relishing in the beauty of his sex.

"Yes," he said.

Her heart constricted, the room suddenly too warm.

"Oh." She didn't want to hear him say he would leave without her. For some reason she couldn't imagine life without him.

Putting her mouth over his cock, she relished the groan that escaped from him. His large hands cupped her head, holding her to him. She ran her hands up his chest, burying her fingers in his chest hair. If this were to be the last time she fucked him, she would make the most of it.

Dammit. She wouldn't think about that now.

Samantha sucked his cock into her mouth, the soft velvety skin moving over the hardened steel of his shaft. She closed her eyes when his grip tightened on her hair.

"I thought you wanted to talk." His voice was scratchy, garbled, aroused to the point where the beast in him struggled to be free.

Raising her head, lifting herself over him, she straddled him, pressing his shaft against the length of her heat.

"But we can talk later," he encouraged, smiling, reaching for her.

"I want to go with you." She couldn't believe her boldness, the words out of her before she could think about them.

"I want you to go with me, too." He didn't hesitate in answering, his expression intent while he adjusted her over his cock.

Something broke inside of her, tension and uncertainty washing through her while happiness overwhelmed her.

"What did you say?" She froze above him, wanting to make sure she understood his words.

"Did you think I would leave here without you?" He smiled, then gripped her hips and impaled her with his cock.

"Oh, God." She arched, closing her eyes, throwing her head back and grabbing her head. "Oh, Johann."

She sunk down onto his cock, burying him inside her, feeling him fill her. All of her worries, her fears that he didn't want her by his side washed through her with her orgasm.

Bracing her legs she lifted herself over him, his cock stroking her insides as she rose over him. She took control, sinking back onto him, riding his cock while she filled herself with him. Every bit of him.

"I didn't know what to think," she whispered, coming down on top of him.

His arms came around her, holding her to him, his heart pounding between her breasts. She moved her hips, building momentum, allowing him to appease an itch she hadn't been able to scratch until now.

Lights seemed to explode around her even though the room was dark. His hands brushed over her, stroking her back the way his cock stroked her insides. She found his mouth, kissing him with everything she had. He tightened his grip, the muscles in his arms flexing, consuming her. She couldn't get enough of him, riding him harder, the friction between them creating a heat that burned through her, cleansing her, lifting all of her worries.

"Samantha." His voice sounded desperate but she couldn't stop, couldn't slow down.

Fire burned inside her, spreading over her. Her legs burned, the muscles constricting from riding him, but she couldn't stop, couldn't ease up.

"Damn, woman." He grabbed her rear end, holding her into place while he drove into her. "Is that what you need?"

"God, yes."

He thrust upwards, taking over, moving in and out of her faster than she had been capable of doing. Rushes of molten heat devoured her, burning her senses, branding her from their heat.

She exploded, fireworks going off around her while heat exploded throughout her body. Rush after rush of fiery moisture surged through her. His hot explosion inside her molded them together, fusing them for life.

"I'm never going to let you go," she warned him, openly admitting for the first time what she'd known for quite a while now.

"You better not." Johann pulled her up to him.

She slid to his side, their sweaty bodies making it to easy to glide off of him.

"Johann?" she whispered, glancing up into his deep blue eyes. Blonde curls stuck to his forehead, his expression intent as he looked down at her. "I need to know how you feel."

He raised his hand and ran a finger down her cheek. "I love you, too, sweetheart."

She almost couldn't swallow. *Too? As in also?* Then heat flushed over her when she remembered her dream. She had told him she loved him, and then had worried that she had spoken out loud.

"You already knew how I felt," she said, knowing now that was why she never sensed worry on him. He'd already known that he had her, that she was his.

"You've told me in your dreams." He kissed her forehead, and tucked her into him. "Now sleep and dream of me some more. Tomorrow we will make arrangements to leave."

"What about Simone? We can't leave her and Jere here." Samantha knew Simone wanted her daughter close to her father. And it would be nice to know someone if they were headed into new territory.

"Simone and I are from this pack. It will be no problem taking her there, too. She will be able to settle in quickly, and help you get to know everyone."

Samantha nodded. Everything would work out. She relaxed next to him, knowing Rick would throw a fit if he learned she slept here with Johann. But she didn't care. Never again would she be parted from the werewolf she loved.

Also by Lorie O'Clare

ॐ

About the Author

ℬ

All my life, I've wondered at how people fall into the routines of life. The paths we travel seemed to be well-trodden by society. We go to school, fall in love, find a line of work (and hope and pray it is one we like), have children and do our best to mold them into good people who will travel the same path. This is the path so commonly referred to as the "real world".

The characters in my books are destined to stray down a different path other than the one society suggests. Each story leads the reader into a world altered slightly from the one they know. For me, this is what good fiction is about, an opportunity to escape from the daily grind and wander down someone else's path.

Lorie O'Clare lives in Kansas with her three sons.

Lorie welcomes comments from readers. You can find her website and email address on her author bio page at www.ellorascave.com.

Tell Us What You Think

We appreciate hearing reader opinions about our books. You can email us at Comments@EllorasCave.com.

HIDE AND SEEK

ജ

Maybe it's just me, but I love nothing better than a sexy cop story where the hero is not brainless (nor is the heroine) yet they, like most of the rest of us, are still clueless and confused enough to make the story realistic. No one likes times of trouble or of not really knowing where to go or whom to ask to help us. Yet something about reading such a story where the cop hero can save the heroine, slay the dragon (or just kick the bad guy's ass), and then our couple can live happily ever after always makes me smile and feel great. So this book was partly selfish, purely for myself. Yet I'd much rather dedicate it to You, Dear Reader, for enjoying such a tale just as much as myself.

Thanks.

Prologue

✍

Josephine Lomax turned off her small Toyota's headlights and killed the engine. Clearing her throat, she tried for what felt like the millionth time in the last hour to rehearse her little speech.

"So you see, Jonathon," she looked solemnly at her own reflection in the rearview mirror, "it appears as if one of the clients we've been shipping goods to for nearly two years is merely a front for something."

Sighing in disgust, she leaned back in her seat, hating how naïve and pedantic she sounded. She had held the junior accountant position at Wells and Mason Mechanics for over a year now. She was hungry for a promotion—*any* promotion—so that she could begin using her accounting degree in her daily work instead of being a glorified gofer.

Josephine had sweet-talked one of the other accountants into letting her look over the books in preparation for the yearly audit over the long weekend. Tess had been more than willing to let Josephine take the books, as she had a handsome stud and raunchy plans lined up—none of which included staring at a laptop screen for hours on end over the next three days.

Early Friday evening, Josephine had realized something was odd with the accounts, but had been unable to find exactly what triggered her instinct. The accounts all balanced—everything added up to the last penny—but the unerring instinct, which was what originally drew her to accounting, screamed at her that something was wrong.

A few hours of further digging, and a pint of double fudge ice cream, had set her mind spinning. One of the major factories Wells and Mason kept books and records for appeared to be a front—not a working factory at all. The money added up, but the *invoices* she was cross-referencing gave her that fishy smell.

Josephine had immediately called Jonathon Mason, the son of one of the partners and her direct boss. He had been shocked and surprised at her news, and had insisted she come over to his apartment with the laptop and printouts and explain her findings straight away.

Josephine tried to quash the niggling sensation that this was a dumb idea. *Don't be stupid, woman,* she reassured herself. *Jonathan is your boss, the son of the man who jointly owns this company.*

Even with this oh-so-logical reasoning, her funny feeling refused to give way. She cringed as that other inner voice, the one insisting something was wrong with the accounts and invoices, piped up again.

Anyway, you have that photocopy and burned CD in your desk if anything really is wrong.

Deciding to ignore *both* the voices talking in her head, Josephine resolutely picked up her briefcase and laptop case, and climbed out of the car. Locking it and heading over to the apartment complex, she walked directly in the bright light, hoping to chase the shadows in her mind away. When she came to the buzzer for Apartment 6, Jonathon's expensive apartment, there was a small sticky-label note attached to it.

Needed more privacy. Go to the swings in park opposite. JM

Josephine turned around and saw a large, dark park over the road. Her gut sank, and all her previous fears about the intelligence of this mission came crashing back. And what could he mean by needing more privacy? How much more private could one get than one's apartment?

Josephine took a deep breath. Obviously he had a woman in the apartment, or maybe the walls were thin. A thousand rational, obvious solutions came to mind. She needed to cut down her reading of romantic thrillers. There was nothing ominous about Jonathon wanting to meet her in a park, for heaven's sake.

Despite her steadying talk to herself, years of reading detective novels and spy thrillers couldn't be deterred. Still determined to do the right thing, but a lot more cautious and wary now, Josephine headed toward the park. Unlike her crossing the parking lot of the apartment building, this time Josephine hid in the dark shadows, hoping to find out what stupid game Jonathon was playing. If he were merely trying to be dramatic or frighten her, she would scream bloody murder at him—boss or no boss.

With the books not tallying correctly just before a major audit, she felt she had a right to be suspicious and on edge, no matter what her position in the corporate hierarchy.

As she tried to walk through the shrubbery and flowers as quietly as possible, Josephine heard a heated, half-whispered conversation occurring. It was coming from a semi-darkened clearing off the proper walking path, but enough light shone through the trees for her to recognize one of the two men.

"Look, Petrelli, I still think this is a bad idea. Lomax is the bottom of the bottom. She's really a coffee girl. She can't possibly know what's going on. Anyway, even if she does blab some nonsense to the other accountants—or anyone else—who's going to believe her insinuations when I step in and cover our tracks? Dad will never believe I can do anything wrong, and he certainly won't listen to some fresh-faced recent college graduate over me. I think you're seriously over-reacting."

The other man spoke much more quietly. Josephine crept closer, trying to hear his words instead of just the low murmur of his voice. As her eyes adjusted to the darkness, she could see Jonathon clearly, his expensive Italian slacks pressed and still crisp after a long day's work, his shirt and tie immaculate.

The other man wore dark clothing, and stood partially hidden to her sight behind Jonathon.

Suddenly, Jonathon moved two paces back giving Josephine a clear view of the other man.

"Whoa!" Jonathon cried out. "You never said anything about making anyone disappear. We might be involved a little in drugs, but murder is way too serious, man!"

Josephine froze, her stomach clenching in fear. She silently ducked even lower into the covering shrubs and bushes. Feeling her back and face start to sweat, she tried not to panic. She had always loved the game of hide and seek as a child. She particularly loved hiding right under the finder's nose, as they so rarely looked close to themselves first. Suddenly, hide and seek took on a whole new meaning. Not only did she feel totally vulnerable in the darkness, but she also worried that the light shrubbery would not hide her to their eyes if they looked carefully.

Her eyes now properly adjusted to the light, Josephine felt her body sweat even more as she finally took in the full ramifications of the second man with Jonathon. He wore a regulation black police uniform and badge. He held his hat in one hand, the other rested on his hip, as if he used the aggressive stance to lend weight to his words.

Josephine was close enough to hear his words now, but they chilled her to the core. She squatted, her laptop clutched so tightly to her chest she feared she would permanently crush her breasts. She froze in the bushes, too scared to move or breathe.

"Listen, you little preppy shit, it might be good enough for you to run off to Daddy for help and asking for forgiveness, but some of us have a lot more at stake here. I've been using that factory for far more than just your petty nose habit. I've had meetings there, hidden people there. I'm not going to give it up just when I'm making a name for myself in certain circles, simply because you're having a case of the scaredy-cats. I don't care what you do to this girl or how you shut her up, but I'm serious. Make this problem go away, and make it go away for good. If you can't scare the shit out of her, I will, and my methods will be far more permanent ones. Understood?"

Jonathon nodded mutely, and Josephine stared at the dirty cop. She memorized his every feature, from his short, regulation-cut black hair, to his flat, scary, dark brown eyes. She looked at his ears and the set of his jaw, and squinted, wishing she could see his badge number. Before she could even hope to discern the numbers, the cop strode away with long, powerful strides, anger etched in his face, and determination in the harsh set of his body.

Josephine, still hugging the heavy laptop and briefcase closely to her, waited for the man to resume his beat patrol. Once he was clearly out of sight, and Jonathon started swearing and pacing, glancing at his watch every few seconds, she silently crept back to where she had left her car. Grabbing a tissue from the car-pack she always kept in the glove box, she hastily, but thoroughly wiped the folders and computer down. Way too many detective and forensic shows had taught her that fingerprints could be dangerous. She wasn't exactly sure how they could prove dangerous to her here, but the simple process of wiping the items down soothed her a little.

Leaving the files and laptop on the doorstep into the apartments, totally uncaring if Jonathon or someone else now picked them up, Josephine rushed back into her car.

Being careful not to speed, since the last thing she wanted was to draw the attention of the police, she drove back to her apartment and packed. Making a few quick phone calls to friends who could monitor the situation both at work and in the local media, she packed a suitcase shoving the CDs full of information and photocopies of the accounts into the side pocket. Her first stop would be to an all-night copy center, where she could pay to burn duplicate copies of the CDs and the accounts. Remembering to pay the following few months rent on her apartment at the last moment, mentally cringing at the depletion of her already-shaky bank balance, Josephine was out her door in next to no time.

Getting into her car once again for the evening, Josephine desperately tried to think of a safe place to head. With nowhere else coming to mind, she pointed the car in the direction of Montana, her childhood home state. She had many fond memories of growing up there, and even now all these years later, she instinctively felt the safety that lay there for her.

Quashing the latter memories of burying both her parents in that very same state, she remembered the warm, safe feeling of being home and loved. Not knowing or even caring exactly where she would end up, she began to drive.

* * * * *

Three months later, somewhere in Montana

Josephine sat in the dingy bar and stared sadly down into her light beer. She grimaced as she took a sip and wondered, not for the first time over the last three months, what the hell she was doing.

Avoiding that creepy, dingy boarding house you're staying in, came the mental reply.

Josephine sighed again and took another sip of the truly awful beer. Her realization was sad, but unfortunately true. She, Josephine Lomax, was most definitely avoiding the rat hole she currently called home. On her way back from her twelve-hour shift in a borderline seedy café where she had found a job as a waitress, she had decided to stop off at a slightly less seedy-looking bar to relax, unwind from her hard day, and kill some time before she collapsed in bed from exhaustion.

So here she sat, surrounded by dirty, smelly men, sipping a beer she detested, all in the name of not going home.

Kind of depressing when one thought about it too clearly.

The shrill feedback from a microphone pulled her out of her spiraling depression and made her try to focus on the tiny stage through all the smoke. Squinting, she could barely make out in the half-light four, or maybe five, men setting up what appeared to be some instruments.

Smiling for the first time all week, Josephine settled back on her barstool and relaxed. If there was to be music, maybe she could stay for an hour or more. She had sorely missed music, the thrum and beat of a great piece of soft rock or jazz. The quasi-classical crap most of the bars and cafés she worked in hung around the very bottom rung of the ladder of music, generally being very bad background music in the attempts to deter people ripping the place apart.

Even if the band only played half-decently, it would be a massive step up for her and cheer her up immensely. Finally she had found the perfect thing to get her going through the next week.

Josephine squinted and tried her best to catch a glimpse of the men setting up. They seemed to be the band members themselves, joking and laughing with each other under the din of the patrons. Josephine concentrated on them, soaking up anything exciting and different in her life.

Yet none of this seemed to explain the racing of her heart, the thudding excitement pumping in her blood. She brushed her thoughts aside, assuming anything new and exciting and screaming of *normal* would give her exactly the same reaction.

The great examples of eye candy she could view, even through the dim, smoky bar atmosphere had nothing to do with it, she assured herself.

A minute later, when the band seemed to have settled itself, a main spotlight, followed by a second one, shone on the men, illuminating them.

Josephine felt her breath catch. Had she thought half-decent eye candy? She must be going blind! The men were *gorgeous*. Looking about her, she wondered where the hysterical, screaming women were. Surely a band this sexy would have a dedicated fan base of teeny-bopping, skinny, blonde adoring women?

Yet the patrons had not changed, had barely moved as the opening of a well-known rock song began. Dirty, smelly men for the most part, tired, overworked waitresses, desperate for the tips and money they were making. Smoke curled from numerous cigarettes, and other things she didn't want to think about, as the patrons continued to drone on and play cards and pool, pretty much oblivious to the band.

It was as she watched the crowd in wonder at their sheer stupidity and lack of taste that she felt the eyes bore into her.

Turning around quickly, she looked once more at the band, *The Howlers*, as they were billed. The four men playing were all definitely handsome by any standard, maybe even truly deserving of the title drop-dead gorgeous, yet Josephine looked more closely at them.

The drummer seemed to be the leader of the group, calling the timing of the song and steadily searching the bar for…what she didn't know. Someone? Some threat? The saxophone player seemed slightly pissed. He winked at the waitress, raising his eyebrows suggestively. When one particularly young one blushed and nodded at him, he seemed to relax, his temper abated. The vocals man crooned his lyrics, eyeing yet another waitress and blowing a kiss to the one the sax man had already seemed to lay claim to.

It was as her eyes caught the bass guitarist she realized it was he who watched her. As she studied him, memorized his features, she realized the strong similarities between the men could only mean they were related. *Brothers?* She wondered.

The guitarist didn't stop looking at her, couldn't seem to take his eyes from her. She took her time looking him over, wanting to be able to identify him later if trouble should erupt.

Let's be honest with ourselves at least, she chided herself.

Fine. He's absolutely stunning, make-your-panties soaked, drop-dead gorgeous and the best eye candy I've seen in months, since even before I left Seattle. Happy?

The silence in her head had her smiling slightly, the closest she'd come to smiling in a long, long time. The man truly was delectable. It was hard to tell with the drummer sitting down, but she felt certain he was taller than both the guitarist and the saxophone man, and only maybe an inch shorter than the vocals man. He seemed well over six feet, and lean in an athletic way.

Strong, and very sure of himself. He exuded a raw power, different from the drummer, who certainly now seemed to be the eldest and thus in charge, but the guitarist seemed to have his own brand of power. Not the seductive, wicked quality both the vocal and sax men held, but a quiet, rock-like strength.

The bass guitarist caught her staring. When her eyes clashed with his, he grinned hugely, the smile lightening his face and making him seem like some sort of playful god. Strong, self-assured, with a steady, rock-like quality to him. Josephine shook her head. Maybe the light beer tasted awful, but she couldn't possibly be tipsy from the few sips she had taken over the last half hour or so.

The man's smile was so infectious, so genuine, Josephine couldn't help herself, she smiled right back at him, her normal, cheery, devil-may-care grin that always made her feel cheeky and wicked. The man studied her further for a moment and then nodded his head, as if he had decided something. He winked at her and paid no attention when the vocals man slapped him on the shoulder in that manly, playful way brothers often have.

The time from then on seemed to pass in a happy, carefree blur. Josephine no longer cared that the bar stank, that the beer tasted repulsive or that the clientele was not exactly safe. She sat and watched the four men interact and jibe each other, singing to the crowd and entertaining themselves, if not some of the patrons.

After their set, the tall bass guitarist headed towards her. His stride, confident and strong, made her quiver, whether in nerves or excitement she didn't know, and didn't particularly care, either.

He glared at the man next to her until he mumbled something rude and shifted to the next barstool away from her.

The man sat down and grimaced at her beer.

"It's awful stuff, I know. I do not recommend it at all." She stopped, wanting to kick herself the second the words left her mouth. Surely he wouldn't be stupid enough to think she was warning him away or something? Before she could rush on and make a bigger fool of herself, her guitarist smiled and spoke to the bartender.

"A Coke for me and the lady will have...?"

Josephine smiled at him. "A white wine spritzer please."

The man nodded at the bartender, who shrugged and moved to get the drinks.

"I'm William Rutledge. What are you doing in such a dive?"

Josephine smiled. If she hadn't spent the best part of the last hour watching him interact with his brothers, she'd be pissed at his bluntness. Yet she had learnt a bit about him in the last hour.

He was a bit rough around the edges, one of those men who used gruffness and blunt, tactless comments to show he was concerned or cared. As she would never see him again and didn't really want to pick a fight, she decided to verbally spar instead of start a drag-out fight with him.

"Not that it's any of your business," she glared at him, certain her smile would soften the blow, "but I just needed a breather before I went back to my motel room. I'm fairly new in town and didn't realize what sort of place this was. By the time I did, my beer was already bought, and I refused to waste four bucks, no matter how awful the beer is. When you and your brothers began to set up, I wanted to stick around for the music. It's been a while since I've heard a live band, and the temptation was too good to resist. Do you often play in rat holes like this?"

The bartender set their drinks in front of them, and Josephine watched William take out a few bills and passed them over with a nod.

"My brothers and I play in any number of bars, ones much classier than this, and sad to say, much worse than this." He shrugged.

Josephine smiled and took a sip of her wine. Just barely, she managed not to choke on it. It was *terrible*. Smiling with a little less brightness, she wondered if she could duck into the restroom and rinse her mouth out with water. She crinkled her nose. Undoubtedly the restroom would be just as dodgy as the rest of the bar.

"Wine not that good, huh?" William smiled gently. When he reached out to touch her thigh, even covered by the black work pants she wore, she felt the electric current run through her, jazzing her as no alcohol or drug ever could.

"What's happening?" she asked quietly, not even really sure what she was asking. The words had somehow seemed to slip out.

William leaned forward, wrapping one arm around her shoulder and drawing her into his warmth.

"I think we have what is generally called an electric reaction. We're inordinately attracted to one another, and we are generating a heap of lust and emotions. What's your name?"

The privacy, the safety and sanctuary she felt in this man's embrace, a feeling she had not felt at all in any form since that fateful night, enveloped her. She felt lightheaded and dizzy, wondered for a moment if she was about to pass out.

The warmth emanating from this man, the potent feeling that he would keep her safe and shield her from all her troubles was more intoxicating than anything else.

"Jose—"she caught herself just in time, "Joey, Joey Lane." She stammered, shocked to the core she was about to tell him her real name. What was happening to her?

William looked down at her for a moment, his deep, deep blue eyes considering.

"Well, Joey," he finally said huskily, his voice deepening with his emotions, "will you come home with me tonight?"

Josephine couldn't believe the desperation with which her body and mind craved to say yes. She was tired, cold, and hungry. She was sick of running, sick of hiding. She hated the life she seemed to have carved out for herself, yet she couldn't see a safe way out of it. Her logical mind argued this was *not* the time to start an affair.

Yet how could she turn down one night of romping, make-your-panties-wet-screaming sex with this man?

Biting her lip softly, she decided to bargain.

"One night?" she offered tentatively. William's eyebrow rose in shock. Josephine frowned. Surely this man had offers all the time? With his looks, and the deadly sexiness of his brothers she felt sure he must have women throwing themselves at him constantly. Surely *some* of the women only wanted one-night stands? Before she could really think about it, she learned another important part of William's character. The man knew how to bargain.

"One night with me getting the option to convince you into a second."

Josephine weighed the pros and cons. She was scared and running. It was highly unlikely *anything* William could say or do would convince her into a second night.

Looking once more into his face, feeling the warmth of his caring and body heat cover her, she made a snap decision — very unlike her — and nodded.

"One night," she warned.

William leaned forwards and kissed her. Josephine felt her whole body heat up and explode. Her body temperature went through the roof. His lips, though so very, very soft, pressed against hers, transferred his heat directly into her. His tongue slipped out and laved her lips, begging for entrance.

With a groan she complied, opening her mouth for his possession. Josephine blinked, realized he had drawn her into his embrace and was shielding her from the patrons, from prying eyes. Melting in his arms, against his so-warm chest, Josephine groaned and deepened the kiss, flicking her tongue out to taste him. She simply couldn't resist.

All too soon, she felt William pulling away. Reluctantly, slowly, with nipping little kisses being strewn over her lips and cheeks.

"I'm sorry, baby, I didn't mean to do all that here. You're like a drug in my system."

Josephine smiled, "A drug, huh? That's not very romantic for a man with only one night."

William seemed to signal the drummer who throughout the whole break had stayed by the edge of the stage, watching the band gear and...was she really this paranoid? Watching out for his band-mates? The other two brothers seemed to have disappeared out back with some of the waitresses.

"My elder brother, Artemais," he said simply, nodding his head towards the man and gave a few quick, easy-to-miss-if you-weren't-watching hand gestures.

With that, he took her coat from the back of the stool and held it out for her.

Smiling, Josephine turned her back and let him help her into it. As he gently pulled it over her shoulders, he leaned down to whisper in her ear, "And that's one night with the option of convincing you of a second. I can be very persuasive, baby."

Josephine shuddered at the warmth emanating from him, at the husky, sexy tone of his voice. She turned to look at him. He stood proud and tall, like a knight out of some erotic fairy tale. He was sex personified and she couldn't wait to begin their one night.

"You might be persuasive, but I'm not some meek little girl. I can handle you."

He grinned a huge, feral, toothy grin.

"I can't wait to see you try. Let's go back to my place, it's not too far from here and I can give you a lift back to your motel room afterward if it'll make you feel better."

Josephine nodded. She couldn't tell how she knew, but she was safe with this man. Her instincts had proved her true and right to date, no sense in ignoring herself just now. She might doubt herself sometimes, but never really her intuition. She just had to remind herself she could only linger and indulge in the one night.

"One night," she reminded herself and him. His grin widened.

"We'll see." He laughed. Waving to his brother, he escorted her out.

Josephine felt excitement tingle her every nerve and the rapid beat of her heart. She deserved this night and this man, and then she would move on.

* * * * *

William didn't know what it was about this woman, but she seemed such a contrary mixture of things. She was obviously classy, but dressed in old, rather worn clothes. She hung out in a total dive he would never have expected any woman to be drinking in, and she seemed so wary of him he couldn't help but feel protective of her. His instincts told him she had a very long, involved story behind her, yet he felt far more interested in stripping her naked and indulging himself in her body and scent than anything else. Plenty of time for questions later, his libido assured him.

He in no way questioned his confidence in convincing her to stay for a couple of weeks. Lately that's all he'd been able to keep interest in any one woman. He enjoyed women, would rather cut his leg off than hurt one, yet he couldn't help but grow a bit weary of constantly being unfulfilled with them.

He knew this woman would be no different, knew she would be simply another person to pass the time with. Yet something about her felt…different. He couldn't really put his finger on it.

He smiled down at her as he led her into his apartment, determined to share most of his secrets and find out all of her own, and then they could move on and see where they led.

* * * * *

Two weeks later.

He's a COP! Her brain screeched at her. Gently, carefully, Josephine extracted herself from the large, warm, comforting embrace. William had come to be the one bright spot in her increasingly frustrating life.

Contrary to her original plans, William had somehow seduced her into more than the one night she had promised herself. One night had become two. Two had become three, and before she had known it they were sharing brunch a week and a half later planning a real, honest-to-goodness date, not just a multiple screaming-when-they-came sexual marathon.

They had gone out to dinner, chatted ordinary small talk for a few hours, and then raced each other to bed. They simply set the sheets on fire, daring each other to go further, to do more. She simply couldn't get enough of his body. He was her physical refuge.

Then late last night, still bloated on his success at gaining a real-live date with her, he had asked her about her work.

When she had smiled and replied that there wasn't anything very interesting about being a waitress in an almost-seedy cafe, he had looked almost bashful. She asked him what he did, and when he replied that he was a cop, she had frozen, totally blindsided.

William had chattered happily for a time, while Josephine pulled herself together. After they had made fierce love, Josephine tried to stifle her tears. She would need to move on again, she really should have done it ages ago.

She had trouble answering to Joey, which she had been calling herself in Montana. She had finally confessed to William that her full name was Josephine, simply so she would pay attention when he called her name. The elaborate web of lies and partial truths she had set up for herself was mostly intact, but she was certain that William knew her too well now to be deceived for much longer. Strange how this man knew her better after approximately two weeks than all her years-long friendships back in Seattle knew her.

In fact, William seemed to simply stare at her every now and then, as if trying to read her thoughts and secrets. It didn't weird her out as it might have in another man— yet she knew sooner or later he would ask questions she wasn't sure she felt ready to handle answering. William, though she mostly knew of him in a sexual sense, was an upright, honest man who seemed to genuinely always want to do the right or best thing. In bed, he was a fierce, consuming lover who always gave her satisfaction.

He had a slightly animalistic streak, which surprisingly, totally turned her on. Considering her usually tame taste in men—almost to the point of boredom—she sometimes questioned her sanity for feeling comfortable with this man. Even so, the inherent safety she felt with him overcame any and all of her doubts.

Yet somehow at the same time, Josephine wasn't exactly sure what William would do if he found out the woman he had been sleeping with was actually an alleged criminal who had a warrant on her head for questions with relation to drug charges. Where they even got the alleged evidence was beyond her. She didn't believe he would be very understanding about it, yet neither was she sure he would throw her out on the streets and join the hunting party. It was confusing and Josephine simply didn't know how she felt about it all.

As the light of dawn started to penetrate the sky, Josephine collected her clothes scattered all across the comfortable room. If her worst nightmares came true, if William did feel honor bound to turn her in, to take the cop's side of the story, she wasn't sure she could survive the heartbreak. Worse would be how he would react to learning she hadn't been fully truthful with him from the start. *That* she felt certain, if nothing else, would upset him. She didn't think she could bear seeing the disgust, the condemnation in William's eyes if she tried to explain her plight to him, undoubtedly digging herself deeper and deeper into the mess.

It was simply easier to move on. She always had her bags half-packed in her closet. She kept her cash wrapped safely in envelopes and stashed in a few secure places, in case she had to run suddenly.

While she knew this wasn't the same sort of emergency she had faced all those months ago, Josephine knew she had to move out of town and quickly, before she felt too burdened with her pain and problems and talked herself into confiding in William.

Taking one last look at the gorgeous sleeping man behind her, Josephine blew him one more kiss, her eyes soaking up his body and relaxed posture, his long hair spread over the still-warm spot she had laid in beside him. Blinking away her stupid tears, she silently apologized once more to him and closed the door sadly behind her.

Chapter One
Six months later

§⟩

"They're *what*??"

"Twins," the nurse repeated, still looking at the ultrasound monitor. Without even glancing at her patient, she leaned closer into the monitor. "Would you like to know their gender?"

Josephine drew in a couple of deep breaths. The last thing she needed was to start hyperventilating and have the nurse bring in a doctor or two who would want to run more tests. Firmly steadying the quivering in her stomach, Josephine barely registered what the nurse said.

"Yeah, sure," she replied, not even certain what she was answering. *Twins*, still echoed in her brain, mocking her.

How could she continue hiding with *two babies*? She had been daunted enough with the thought of keeping one child safe in her strange new life. Her savings account was totally drained, so the thought of feeding and clothing *two* babies on the meager salary she earned as a waitress did nothing to help calm her nerves.

She fiercely wished she could go back to accounting, to earn a decent wage again. The shiny, wonderful thought of being able to rely fully on herself without the constant pressure she had been facing over the last few months almost made her mouth water. But the thought of having her name circulating back in the accountancy circles was enough for a fresh wave of fear to crash over her.

With the warrant still out for her questioning, she was far too scared of being dragged back to Seattle, and she couldn't get a decent job under a false name without her credentials.

Her degree and all her memberships were under her real name, not the pseudonym she now used.

Josephine sighed. She had finally become accustomed to answering to Joey Lane, but the indignity of using a false name and living from her cash-in-hand waitressing was getting tiresome. Plus her boss had started talking rather loudly about how pregnant women were supposed to stay at home, eat, and get fat more quickly than she was. He had a fundamental problem with a six months pregnant mother-to-be working on tables.

Josephine knew she would be pounding the pavements again soon looking for work, or she wouldn't be able to afford the shabby but clean boarding house room she had found. In fact, she could hardly believe her luck when they hadn't bothered to check her ID, finding such luck twice in a row was more than even *she* would believe in.

Yet again, for the zillionth time since she had crept out in the pre-dawn light, Josephine thought of William and the possibility of returning to him. She had left the city constantly looking over her shoulder, as she had a number of times since that fateful night, always hiding, never staying long in one place.

Yet whenever she felt most scared, whenever she was certain she couldn't continue this farce, she thought of William and the temporary safety she had felt in his arms. The tenderness and yes, even love, she had felt in his embrace.

Josephine sighed at her soft thoughts. Maybe it really was time to stop running and confront her fears. She certainly couldn't continue as she had been with two babies, she really couldn't have done it even with one baby. Maybe she should go back and talk to William. Much as she hated to admit it, she had probably overreacted to his being a cop. She couldn't see him throwing her out to be murdered or abused by anyone, pregnant or not.

As badly as she wanted to believe and fantasize that William would take her in, hold her close and protect her, a much smaller, half-hidden part of her still scorned herself for her fantasy. She couldn't begin to count the number of times she had held a public phone, desperately craving to call him, to hear his voice, both before and after she had found out she was pregnant. Yet because she couldn't be certain of his reaction to her plight, she had always hung up the phone in disgust with herself for her lack of courage. She stubbornly clung to relying on herself, depending on herself, and not the man whom she cared for more than she should.

Even after she had found out about the baby, *babies* she mentally corrected herself, she hadn't wanted to simply turn up on William's doorstep and lean on him. She had always been self-reliant, sufficient in and of herself. Turning to a man simply because she was pregnant galled her beyond belief.

And so she had been stubborn and pigheaded and refused to turn to the one man who wouldn't abuse her trust. William had so much strength he always seemed to expect everyone around him to lean on him. Josephine supposed that in itself was part of her reason for refusing to cling to him. She was a modern woman, used to relying on herself.

Now she was supposed to be adult enough to see to not only her own needs, but also be responsible for those of her twins. It was the latter responsibility that weighed on her. She didn't mind doing stupid, stubborn things when only she would pay the consequences. Surely it was better for her to swallow her pride and ask William for help? She didn't have to live with the man or anything, she could just ask for his opinions, get his advice on what she should do.

Josephine smiled sadly. It had taken an ultrasound and the reality of seeing her two little babies to make her realize what she should have known six months ago. She could not only trust William, but returning to him wasn't relying on him as such, it was *sharing* herself and her burden.

She didn't need to turn into some sappy spineless woman simply because she had turned to a man for help. They could work something out together as equals.

112

Josephine frowned. It made a hell of a lot of sense, but in the confusion of the last few months her perspective seemed to have changed. She was no longer the completely cool, logical thinker she had always assumed she was.

"...yes, definitely two boys, see that? There, and there, definitely two very fine young men you're carrying, Ms. Lane."

Josephine finally tuned back in to the gushing nurse. *Twin boys*, she thought, her heart lifting slightly, her deep contemplation diverted for now. Two happy, healthy young men, who would probably be the very image of their father and steal her heart the instant she laid eyes on them.

"So, Ms. Lane, looks like you got the two-for-one deal," the nurse chirped, taking away the ultrasound. "Two little boys, probably identical you realize, though we can't be sure, of course. Your partner will be so happy."

Josephine felt a pang of guilt; William really should have been here with her to experience this. Not for the first time Josephine wondered if being pregnant had scrambled her brains. Her usually logical, practical brain had seemed to leave her when she drove away from Seattle. Everything seemed such a mess. Feeling the crushing burden fall back on her shoulders after the lightness she had wallowed in with her unborn sons, Josephine knew she needed to go back to her small but clean room back at the boarding house and think more about her predicament.

Maybe Adam would be around. Adam was the scraggly bellboy-cum-errand boy the boarding house employed. They had become fast friends when she first arrived, tired and sick, the third month of her pregnancy making her so ill she wished for death.

Adam had made a joke, insinuating she looked so battered and worn because she was running from the mob, the boss of which had knocked her up. When Adam had gallantly offered to marry her and save the life of her unborn child, she had laughed and they had chatted over hot chocolate, instantly becoming good friends.

Maybe finally confessing the full story, not the partial story she already had confided to Adam, and asking his opinion on what she should do would give her a fresh perspective on everything. Adam knew full well her opinions on relying on anyone other than herself. Although Adam was not the most logical, practical person she had encountered, her own scrambled thought processes might return with his helpful input.

Josephine knew that Adam liked her just for being herself, and she loved him in return like a little brother. Even though he was a few years her senior, he acted so much like a horny teenager that it was hard to see him in any sense other than a rascally little brother. The knowledge that it wasn't just her life she was now organizing, but those of her sons as well, lent a far more serious note to her contemplations.

She sighed. Refusing to feel guilty over how long it had taken her to shape up and recognize she couldn't do this alone anymore, she adjusted her clothes as the nurse finished cleaning the ultrasound equipment.

Yes, she would return to the boarding house and chat to Adam in her small room. He always had a joke or two to cheer her up, and when she could convince him to get serious, his opinions meant a lot to her. Taking the hand the friendly nurse was offering, she climbed off the small, cramped bed and finished rearranging her clothes.

Heading out into the chilly Montana wind, Josephine pulled her coat tighter around her rather large belly. Keeping her head down, she headed back the short distance to the house. Checking her watch, she knew Adam should be around. The thought of some hot chocolate along with a good long chat with her dear friend spurred her to walk faster in the cold day. She knew a good long talk would help her sort her mind out, but a sinking part of her knew already both what her friend would say and what she would end up doing.

Return to William.

It was the right thing to do. Even though she would never feel bad about the last few months she had learned to live alone and the confidence she had built in herself, Josephine knew she should have headed straight back to William as soon as she had seen the positive pregnancy tests.

All three of them.

She would talk to Adam, confide the whole story to him. Josephine felt her stomach tighten and turn over as her babies played inside her.

Returning to William. Josephine felt excited and scared simultaneously.

Chapter Two

∞

"What do you mean you're not sure? Dammit, Samuel, we've been searching for *months*! I thought you were this hot-shot private eye?"

William Rutledge paced the length of the comfortable inner-city office his younger brother, Samuel, used as his base for his private investigations firm. Running an agitated hand through his long, dark brown hair, he resisted the impulse to start pulling the strands out or to open the window and start baying in frustration out into the street below.

It had been six very, very long months since he had woken up alone that first time. Originally, he had been piqued, depressed over how Josephine could have left him without a note or even a simple, "See you around, it's been fun." When he had finally confessed his depression and anger to his new sister-in-law, Sophie, after two weeks of angst and anger, he had realized that there might have been more to Josephine's leaving than he realized.

Sophie, his elder brother Artemais' new wife and mate, had pointed out that Josephine might have been running, or scared, or any number of horrible things he didn't want to contemplate. Sophie had gently urged him to dig a little into her background and find out what really was happening.

When he had performed a cursory police check into Josephines from the Seattle area, including her vital stats and the scanty tidbits of information he had gleaned about her over the two weeks they had been seeing each other, he had found some rather disquieting news. There was a warrant for questioning out on one Josephine Lomax, from the outer Seattle area. Even though the surname wasn't that of his

Josephine, the physical description and rough time of leaving the area fit his woman perfectly.

William hadn't believed for a moment that his Josie dabbled in drugs, in any sense. But the fact that she had a warrant out on her head made him worried for her. Why was she running? He *knew* there was a misunderstanding somewhere, but why not explain to the police what was going on? Why run, when it made her look so guilty?

The questions had been whirling around in his head for all these long, cold months, and the more time that stretched by, the more worried he became. He surreptitiously checked daily in the logs and records of the Seattle branch of police where the warrant originated.

No one anywhere seemed to have heard from her, so he at least had the consolation that no one else had found her. But that left a set of different worries in his head.

Was she hurt? Was she cold? Hungry? The frustration he felt at not being able to help her, protect her, was driving him nuts. He felt proud that she was so independent, and so frustrated at the same time he felt like roaring out his anger or at the very least kicking something inanimate. Hard.

"Are you even listening to me, bro?"

"Huh?" William turned back to where Samuel, two years his junior, was leaning back in his old-fashioned padded chair. "Of course I was listening. Sort of. Maybe want to repeat it?"

Samuel sighed disgustedly, and put his fedora hat back on his head, his detective pose back in place.

"I said your chick is obviously living on cash. Her bank accounts had a couple of hefty withdrawals on the night she ran, but since then no money has come in or out of them. She hasn't re-registered with any of her Accountancy clubs, so it's unlikely that she is working a proper full-time job. Unless your girl knew beforehand that she would be running and has set up a full and proper set of alternate credentials —"

"No, no," William interjected. "She didn't have any details or accounts under Joey Lane, she often didn't even respond to the name at the start of our relationship. I really think this was a spur of the moment thing that just stretched on and on since the warrant was released."

William ignored the slightly pitying glance Samuel gave him.

"You've got it bad, bro. I want to find this chick even more than you do simply so I can see what kind of woman can have you tied up in knots like this. The only other interesting tidbit I'm inclined to share is that Petrelli, the guy in charge of the investigation, recently left Seattle. He was just promoted to Detective and got assigned to the case. Then he filed for a month's leave a couple of days ago. I have no idea if it's important, I'm just keeping you up to date. I do have a few other semi-leads, but I want to see how they pan out, and it's getting late. What say we hit the bar, meet up with Dom and have a night out?"

William wasn't much in the mood for partying, especially the style of partying Samuel and Dominic would probably do in the bar. Dominic was the youngest and certainly wildest of the four brothers. William's taste for casual flings and one-night stands had never been strong, and had become nonexistent since he met Josephine.

Yet, neither did he really want to return to his large home where he lived with his three brothers and new sister-in-law. Artemais and Sophie had only just had baby Christiana, and while he loved his little niece, he felt restless.

"I think I'll pass tonight, bro. I might just pick up some takeout and it's getting late. I'll chase down a few leads of my own tomorrow before heading back to the house to help Sophie and Christiana settle in. They only came back from hospital the other day."

William smiled and waved at Samuel as he headed out the door, determined to get some more work done tonight.

Collecting some Chinese from the store on the corner, he retrieved his car and drove back to his small but tidy apartment. As he walked down the corridor leading to his apartment, he heard an achingly familiar voice reply loudly, almost in a panic.

"No really, Mrs. Peterson, I'll be fine. I can come back later, really!"

Quickening his pace, he rounded the corner, wishing like hell he hadn't chosen the apartment in the furthest back corner of the floor. He was half-afraid he was imagining her voice, having hallucinations. He dimly heard Mrs. Peterson, bless her soul, insisting the "young lady and her friend" come inside her apartment for a pot of tea and a bit of a sit-down. That he, William, would be back soon undoubtedly, and she would hate for them to wait out in the drafty corridor.

William came around the final corner to where his and Mrs. Peterson's doors were, almost at a run. He worried Josephine would disappear before he could grab her. His legs halted as he saw her, even more beautiful than he remembered. Her shoulder-length auburn hair glowed with the inner reddish-brown color of a delicious flame.

He loved her hair, had spent hours staring and brushing it when they had spent quiet evenings after intense lovemaking. As she heard his approach, she had turned to him, and he felt his breath freeze when he stared into that lovely, heart-shaped face. The green eyes he had dreamt about for months were sadder, lonelier than he remembered. He desperately wanted to bring that mischievous sparkle back into them that he knew could be present.

And then he felt his mouth gape as he saw her *huge* belly and much fuller breasts.

Oh my Lord, she's pregnant! Largely pregnant. Is it…?

He left the incredibly masculine and possessive thought of *Mine* untouched. He didn't want to get his hopes up. After six cold, lonely months of contemplation he half-reasoned she *had* to be his True Mate.

It would certainly explain a few things, like how he could never, no matter how busy or stressed, get her out of his mind. How he dreamed about her almost nightly. How he loved her scent…and a million other things. Sure, he could have picked up some nameless woman and fucked her raw to try and sate his craving for Josie, but why hurt the poor girl by kicking her out of his bed as soon as he was done? Even the thought of fucking some other woman left a bitter taste in his mouth. He only wanted his Josephine.

Stepping forward, closing the distance between them, he dropped the bags of food on the floor and rested one hand gently, yet possessively over her rounded stomach. Feeling the tiny movements of life, sensing the spirit encased in her womb, he mentally confirmed that she was indeed pregnant. Needing desperately to know if the child was his, he scented her deeply.

Almost drowning in her beloved scent, that one he had craved like a drug in these last barren months, he allowed himself to wallow in the flowery, feminine smell that was uniquely Josephine. He concentrated his senses on the baby, scented himself and Josephine mingled in their baby.

He felt his heart lighten and nearly explode with happiness. Josephine was having his baby, *their* baby. She had to be his True Mate, as no other woman alive could bear his children. For a split second, William blushed, imagining what his brothers, Artemais in particular, would have to say to him.

"You didn't recognize your True Mate? After sleeping with her for two straight weeks and impregnating her? Let's go back over these lessons I taught you twenty-odd years ago…"

Even knowing the verbal and likely not-so-verbal abuse he was likely to cop in the very near future, William still felt as though all his birthdays had come at once. He felt that giant piece of him that had been missing with her absence click back into place.

Now she was his.

He could claim her, mate with her, do all the things he had fantasized about in the dark of night over the last six months. He felt elated, and surrounded his essence around his little child. As he searched, he frowned for a moment, confused. There was another scent, almost identical, yet somehow...

"Twins?!!"

It took him a moment to realize that in his shock and joy he had spoken aloud. William felt his mind spin dizzyingly. He looked back down to Josephine, and the surprise flaring in her eyes.

He dropped his hand and took a step back. Hearing plastic bags rustle, he realized he had dropped his Chinese, now threatening to leak all over the carpet, and he hadn't even been aware of it. Hastily scrambling to collect the bags, smiling as sweetly as possible at Mrs. Peterson, he tried to herd Josephine and her un-looked-at friend into his apartment without making any more mess with the now-useless Chinese.

"Thank you so very much, dear Mrs. Peterson, for looking after my fiancée and her friend. I was running a tad late..."

"What?"

William ignored Josephine's cry, hastily opening his door and shoving the two of them inside before he exploded from pride and curiosity. Barely pausing for a breath, he continued to Mrs. Peterson.

"...and am so glad you kept her here. I'll stop in sometime soon and we can catch up over some tea and those scrumptious scones of yours, hmm?"

The old woman looked sharply at him, consideringly. He felt an overwhelming relief when she nodded, an answering twinkle in her eye.

"Of course, William, I'd love for you to introduce your young lady to me properly. Just leave a note if I happen to be out when you stop by, okay?"

"No problem. Thanks again."

William shut the door and dumped the ruined Chinese on the table. Barely even glancing at it, already having dismissed it from his mind, he strode into the living room, needing to hug and touch Josephine like he needed his next breath. He desperately needed to reassure himself his Josephine really was here.

Chapter Three

ဢ

"What the hell do you mean by calling me your fiancée?"

William leaned over the counter and switched on the kettle. He had a feeling some herbal tea, while not calming Josephine down by any means, might make the situation a little bit easier on them all. As he turned back to face Josephine, he finally saw the friend who had escorted her.

A relatively tall, maybe six-foot to his six-foot-three, young man with bright red hair all mussed, leaned negligently on his windowsill. Dressed casually in blue jeans and a black sweater, he held Josephine's coat over one arm and looked completely at ease.

Searing jealousy caught William by surprise.

"Who the hell are you?" he demanded, startling Josephine and himself at the possessive, angry tone of his voice. The young man, obviously unaffected, smiled for the first time, making his already young features look even younger.

"I'm Adam Carrpen. It's nice to finally meet you, William. As the cliché goes, I've heard lots about you."

William tried to quash the rising green monster inside his body. Turning stiffly to Josephine, he calmly and, he hoped, quietly inquired, "Who the hell is he and why is he here?"

Josephine smiled as she sank down into the soft cushions of his couch. Her gorgeous smile directed at him lightened her face, which eased his jealousy somewhat.

"Adam is a good friend. He works at the boarding house where I've been staying. He didn't want me making the four-hour drive up here alone when there was no guarantee you'd even still be here. So he accompanied me. He knows all about the babies and you, and he's been a very dear friend these past few months. It's actually him you have to thank for convincing me to come back here."

William looked carefully at Josephine. While she didn't look scared, there was an underlying tension in her, in the way she moved and kept looking out the window, as if seeking escape.

"Yeah, man," Adam injected, "I've already offered to marry Josie a dozen or more times. She keeps on turning me down. Personally I think she just doesn't want to marry a glorified bellboy, but she does boost my ego constantly by laughing at my jokes, so it's a rejection I can handle."

Laughing—William was sure—at him, Adam started fixing the tea when the whistle boiled, allowing William to sit gingerly next to Josephine on the couch.

"How did you know they were twins? And how can you tell they're yours? I mean, the fact that I'm here is pretty self-explanatory, but still…"

William smiled and wrapped one arm around her. Relishing the sensation of her leaning against his strength, even just for the moment, he closed his eyes and inhaled her flowery scent one more time.

"It's kind of tricky. Can I get away with just saying I'm special? I want you to eat and get warm, maybe even get a decent night's sleep, before we go into those sorts of explanations. Plus, I think you might have a few answers for me too, hmm?" When she only nodded and settled herself deeper into his embrace, William pulled her tighter, determined not to let her go again.

Adam crossed back over to the couch and handed Josephine a steaming mug of the chamomile tea he had set out. William nodded his thanks to the man.

"You've been watching out for Josephine these past few months?" he asked politely.

Adam shrugged.

"She sorta tends to look after herself, you know? I've talked to her a bit after her shifts down at the diner, haven't I, babe?"

William felt Josephine stir, trying to sit back up properly.

"It's okay, you just relax there. I'm comfortable."

William felt relief when she settled back down and started sipping her tea. Her grimace of distaste made him smile. He watched her eyes fight against drooping. His heart warmed as she reminded him of Christiana, who fought sleep just as determinedly, even when she was obviously exhausted from being awake for a short time.

He reasoned she must be exhausted after such a long car trip, as heavily pregnant as she was. He remembered how Sophie in her last month or two became exhausted after a simple shopping trip, and would sleep for hours afterwards. His Josephine was a strong woman to be able to handle all she did. He couldn't resist stroking her soft hair, soothing her even more. He relished the safety she obviously felt with him.

"Really, William, Adam has been a great friend. He has a wicked sense of humor, and he makes me laugh so loudly sometimes when I really need it. He's sweet and caring. A girl couldn't ask for a better friend. Personally, I think he's one of those Clark Kent types—you know, all sweet and gentle in his normal life, but some sort of superhero after dark. I'm sure there's more to him than he shows people like me. I bet he's this daring cat burglar, or a porn star, or a mobster boss on the side. I'm certain there's this other person lurking deep within him."

Josephine seemed happy to settle into his arms, lean against his chest. She had taken her shoes off when she entered his apartment, and curled her feet under her body. She reminded him for the moment of a contented cat. But like a cat, he was certain she would feel the need to dart and run again when she felt threatened.

Continuing his soothing petting of her hair, William took the chance to look closer at Adam, to study him. He was blushing bright red from Josephine's praise and opinions. He stammered denials of having an alternate life, though neither he nor Josephine listened very much to them. Thinking that there did appear to be more to the man than a first glance would tell, William watched Josephine's cup of tea as her eyes continued to droop. How he had missed her these last few months.

"I think you're right, darling. I think your Adam definitely has hidden depths. But I do think you had better get ready for bed, you look ready to fall asleep right here, and although I certainly wouldn't mind, I'd much rather you slept safely in my bed."

Her eyes widened.

"Your bed? But William—"

"Shh," he cautioned, gently placing one finger over her soft lips. He felt a searing urge to kiss those lips, to lick them and taste them once more. But with her bone-weary with the need to sleep, and her friend standing not three feet away watching him carefully, he didn't want to make a spectacle of them both. He knew once he started kissing his Josephine he wouldn't want to stop.

"Just go on to the bedroom. I'll feed Adam and get him settled on the couch. It pulls out into a bed. I'll come in and check on you later, you just get comfortable, okay?"

William fought the urge to laugh as Josephine looked carefully from him to Adam and then back to him again. Finally her sleepiness won out, and she picked up her small bag and went down the hall to the main bedroom. He heard the door shut and the shower turn on. William crossed over to the linen cupboard and pulled down some sheets and blankets.

"You're more than welcome to spend the night. I'm sorry I was a bit...upset...when I first saw you, but the thought of

Josephine with another man is enough to make me lose my cool."

"No worries, man. Like I said, I'm just a friend. Josie is a cool girl. When she found out her kid was actually twins she nearly dropped her bundle. She came to talk to me about her options, and I finally pressed her on why she'd left you. No offense, but I needed to know if she'd run from you 'cos she was being hurt, or if she'd just got some damn fool notion in her head. When she only half answered my questions, I needed to see her here and safely settled for myself. But I think you'll take care of her, right?"

William looked at the younger man.

"Definitely. She ran out on me without my knowledge. If I'd had even an inkling of an idea she was pregnant, I would never have let her simply disappear by herself. I've been trying to track her down for months. She's not an easy woman to find when she's not interested in being found."

Adam nodded and crossed the room to pick up his small backpack.

"Look, man, I think there's something she's really scared of. I was worried it was you, but it doesn't appear to be that in any sense. She's really scared of something or someone. I don't know and don't particularly care what it is, but you better take good care of her or I swear I'll hunt you down and hurt you."

When William bristled, not liking the challenge, the younger man raised his arms in a soothing, pleading gesture.

"No, no. Don't take me wrong. I like Josie, but she was never sexually interested in me. I'm her friend and always will be. I trust you to take care of her, but I'm just warning you not to abuse that trust of mine. Right? I'm going to head back; I have an early shift tomorrow. Here's how you can get in touch with me if you need a second pair of eyes or something, okay? Josie already has my numbers, so don't worry about that."

William reached out for the scrap of paper with an address and phone number and cell phone number scrawled on it.

"I have three brothers who can help me if I need it, but I do appreciate your offer and will keep it in mind. You sure you don't want to spend the night? Josephine will kill me if she thinks I've thrown you out."

Adam tilted his head, agreeing with his thought.

"I'll just call through the bathroom door that I'm going, so she doesn't worry."

Adam headed off toward the bedroom, knocking on the outer door before creaking it open. William rinsed the cup Josephine's tea had been in and checked his supply of bread and juice, wanting to make sure there was enough for a pregnant, hungry lady and himself the following morning.

He briefly recalled and smiled at how starving his sister-in-law had been throughout her pregnancy. At times, she had even rivaled him and his brothers for the size of her appetite. His elder brother, Artemais, had often laughingly complained she would ruin him by eating so much. He then would ask the stores to make special deliveries, just for them and their appetites.

As Adam came back, whistling cheerily, William thanked the man again for his help and walked him down to the car. Waving him off, he hurried back to the apartment, not wanting Josephine to feel upset at being left alone even for a minute.

Hearing the shower still running as he closed and locked the front door behind him, William smiled as he remembered how Josephine loved to stretch out her shower time. She often simply stood under the hot spray, letting it pound down on her soft body, relaxing her muscles and heating her flesh.

William felt himself harden as images of previous showers shared flitted through his head. Erotic snapshots of himself and Josephine, entwined together as they shared drugging kisses and slow thrusts of lovemaking.

Kicking off his shoes and bending down to pull his socks off, William knew he had to join her in the shower or go completely insane. It had been so many long, lonely months since he had shared anything with Josephine. Even if she wasn't up to some steamy sex, simply being with her, touching her soft skin would help ease the ache that had settled over his heart from the moment he had woken up without her.

Heading towards his bathroom, he swore to himself that he would give her the choice.

If he tried to influence her in one direction, that wasn't his fault, was it?

Chapter Four

Josephine inhaled the masculine scent of William's soap. Funny how she had forgotten some of the smaller things about her man, the scent of his soap, for example. She would never get the scent of his body, of his skin, out of her system, but she had forgotten the slightly different scent of his soap.

Lathering up her arms and chest, she happily hummed under her breath as she surrounded herself with her lover's scent.

She had also missed unlimited hot water. Every shower she had been in, except William's, in all the months she had been running, had a short supply of hot water. She had always loved wallowing in her shower.

As indulgences went, she felt hers was harmless. But oh, how she missed truly taking her time in the shower. With her hair tied up in a bun on top of her head, Josephine felt free to take her time, and as much of the hot water as she pleased, as she soaped her body over and over. Even after all these months, she still felt slightly weird feeling her large belly. Already she felt as large as a house, with the massive protrusion of her stomach.

As surprised as she had been to discover she was carrying twins, it made a strange sort of sense. While she had never thought herself fat, she was certainly curvy. With all this extra weight, both in her breasts and in her stomach, she felt bulky and awkward. Running a hand soothingly over her stomach, she admitted to herself that having two little boys would certainly make up for all the uneasiness and annoyance the pregnancy had brought her.

But what to tell William?

Shivering, even under the hot spray of the shower, she started soaping up her legs and stomach yet again. The simple fact she had returned to him proved that she trusted him, even if he was a cop. But she was unsure just how much she could trust him. After all, she had thought she could trust Jonathon and her bosses, yet that obviously wasn't true. How much did she really know about William, other than he was easily the world's best lover, and now the father of her twin sons?

Her heart insisted he was an honorable man—it was why she had left in the first place. It was her head that held doubts. If it really came down to William believing her, or believing his fellow cops, whom would he trust? Some woman he had slept with months ago who was stupid enough to become pregnant, or his fellow men in uniform?

While these worrisome thoughts rushed around her head, she felt the cold draft of the door opening. Turning around and pushing aside the curtain of the shower, she yelled out, "Go away, Adam! I heard you before. Thank you for driving me here. I'll call you later in the week, okay?"

When a very large, very naked chest came into view, she squeaked and closed the curtain in a hurry.

She knew that chest. Had tasted it many times, felt it over and under her, in almost every position physically possible.

A low, very masculine chuckle came from behind the flimsy curtain.

"Please don't tell me you're shy all of a sudden, Josephine. Shame on you! After all we've shared?"

Feeling her mouth go dry, Josephine saw fleeting images of her favorite moments they had shared together. There were a lot of them. As the curtain moved once again, Josephine stared up into the intensely blue eyes of her lover. Gloriously naked, he stepped into the shower stall.

Her eyes drank in the now-tied-back fall of hair she so loved and had missed so much. It sat up on the back of his head in a half-bun, half ponytail concoction similar to her own

131

mop of hair. His intensely blue eyes burned with a passion she had only ever seen in him.

Soaking up her fill of his exquisite body, she felt her mouth open in shock at the hugely erect cock he wore. He was hard as a pole, and even jutting out from his body, his cock reached up to his navel. Realizing that she was staring, Josephine raised her gaze back to his, only to see him laughing silently at her.

Without his even touching her, she felt the searing heat of his caress, his skin, and his possession. She stared into his face as he wet himself under the hot spray of water. He took the soap from her slack hand, and began to spread it over his long arms and large chest.

Josephine turned her back to him, determined to try and hide her lust and embarrassment. Cupping the heat of the water to her chest, she resisted the urge to duck her head under the spray. When William came across her, covering her body with his large, soapy one, she shuddered in pure bliss.

"You always did love a good, long, hot...shower," he whispered teasingly in her ear. Josephine surprised herself by blushing. She couldn't remember the last time she had blushed like a schoolgirl.

She turned to face the large man in the shower with her, only to find herself cornered against the chilly tiles. William spread his legs to trap her slimmer ones. He reached up and detached the showerhead. Bringing the lovely hot spray down to rain on her quickly chilling flesh, she couldn't bite back the moan of pleasure she felt with the hot, hard spray coming onto her.

"That's it, love," he crooned. "You have no idea how many nights I spent in my bed thinking of you, worrying about you, dreaming of doing this and a million other things to you."

William kept one arm on the moveable shower nozzle. Angling the spray over one nipple, then the other, Josephine didn't pay any attention to his other hand as it grabbed the bar of soap. When he started, oh-so-carefully, to soap up her enormous stomach with such tenderness and patience, she felt a tear form in her eye. How could she have possibly worried, even for a second that this large, gentle man could have, under any circumstances, looked at her with disgust? That he could not have cared for her in any way?

Josephine shook her head in bemusement. Maybe all the hormones running around in her system had fried her brain.

She watched William massage her belly, over and over, a sort of awe and excitement in his eyes she had never seen before. He was so gentle, almost reverent. He moved the showerhead, so it rained down fully on her stomach, rinsing the soap away.

A moment later, William returned the showerhead to its proper position and turned back to crowd her into the tiles. Josephine smiled. She was certain William would look silly to a person looking in on them. His chest pressed into her, crushing her full and sensitive breasts. His legs contained her own and her large belly stuck out into him, making him bend awkwardly over her. Despite the obviously tricky position he was in, he looked so serious, so deeply into her eyes, she didn't dare laugh.

Pressed against the tiles, Josephine looked up into his face as the warm water streamed down his long hair, partly released from his ponytail. Suddenly, when she was sure he would say something as serious as the look in his eyes, William groaned and bent down to kiss her fiercely.

The possession, the fiery claiming in that kiss made her blood hum and sing throughout her body, electrifying long dormant erogenous zones. Josephine felt her legs wobble under the pressure and passion she felt in his kiss, in the strength of his lips claiming hers.

Josephine had read every book she could lay her hands on about sex during pregnancy. She had insisted to herself it was so she could be fully knowledgeable about her pregnancy—but deep, deep inside herself, a part of her just wouldn't quit hoping she would return to William and need the information she had researched.

Not that reading information about it had helped her any. Each different text seemed to contradict itself. All agreed that it was safe for the baby, as it was encased in a liquid-filled sac of sorts. As the sac was filled with fluid, up until the final month or two of pregnancy, even the roughest of penetrations would merely make the baby bounce around. In the final month, sex was one way to induce labor, so most doctors recommended abstaining.

But the sex drive and libido of women seemed to be fiercely debated. Many texts claimed that the hormones produced, testosterone in particular, made women crave sex even more than pre-pregnancy, yet others claimed that some women felt turned off of sex completely until months after the baby was born.

Josephine had been interested, but not worried about her lack of feeling either way. She neither craved sex manically, nor did the thought of sex repulse her. But with William kissing her so ravenously, and the spray of water over her skin, she felt a flush creep up her body until she was canting her hips to better feel his hugely erect cock.

As the one kiss turned into many deep kisses, Josephine heard a low groan. Not knowing or caring whom it came from, she pressed up into William's embrace. Tangling her tongue around his, she teased and tempted him. Darting in to taste him, and share her chamomile taste with him then withdrawing her tongue to make him follow her, she enjoyed their physical play.

As the minutes passed, Josephine finally pulled her lips from his, to begin a long string of caressing kisses down his neck. Taking a playful bite or two along the journey, Josephine took her time and relished the panting breaths William tried to catch in vain.

When she felt his large fingers gently squeeze, then pluck one of her nipples, she sucked in a hasty breath. Her nipples were particularly sensitive, as her breasts had filled out a lot during the last month. While the caress wasn't painful, her tips were so sensitive, the gentle caress bordered on pleasurable pain.

"Oh my," she managed to moan. Hearing William chuckle in male amusement, she opened one eye to glare at him.

"What do you find so amusing?"

William continued plucking and tweaking her nipple, alternating between the two so neither one felt neglected.

"Oh, I've heard that women's breasts become very sensitive during pregnancy. I merely wanted to test the theory, as you seem to be having so much fun taunting me with those sweet lips of yours."

"Know a lot of…oooh…pregnant women huh?"

Josephine started having trouble following the conversation as William bent down to take one nipple in his hot mouth. The shower spray was hot, but William's mouth and teasing tongue were far hotter. Josephine was astoundingly glad that the strength and bulk of William's body pressed her into the wall. Without them, she might easily have slid down to the floor.

"My sister-in-law just had a baby. My brother…teased us all a little sometimes, when his head was particularly swollen."

Josephine laughed, then nearly choked as he bit gently down on her flushed nipple.

"You mean when his lower head finally subsided?"

Surprised and shocked blue eyes pulled away then looked down to her. As she grinned up at him, the shower spray once more hit her full on the breasts and belly, warming her skin up once more.

"I must be losing my touch if you can make double entendres like that while I suck your luscious breasts. Maybe I ought to try a bit *harder*."

With that, William returned his head to her rounded breast, but this time instead of using his hands to play with her other nipple, one hand feathered down to her wet curls. Warm and damp, with both the water and her own creamy juices, she spread her legs for his probing fingers. When two long fingers finally penetrated her heat, she moaned and closed her eyes.

It had been far, far too long.

Almost immediately, William's fingers started pumping in and out of her tight core. His suckling increased, both in intensity and in rapidity. Josephine was shocked to find herself arching up into his mouth, thrusting her hips deeper and deeper onto his long, smooth fingers.

"Are you sure this is safe for the baby?" William muttered against her breast.

"Yeah, sex is fine up to the last month. Surely your brother gloated right until the end?"

Josephine didn't hear exactly what William muttered, but hearing "cocky bastard" gave her the flavor of his reply.

After a few moments of feeling the deep penetration of his fingers, of lifting herself into the nibbling caress of his lips, Josephine cried out from the aching loss of his fingers in her core and his mouth from her breast.

William quickly returned his mouth to hers, murmuring against her kiss-softened lips, "Don't fret dear, we'll take this slowly. I promise."

When Josephine was about to insist she didn't *want* to take this slowly or delicately, she felt the very tip of William's cock sit at the entrance to her pussy. With her lips pressed tightly against his, and the very tip of his head inside her, Josephine felt as if she had finally arrived home.

She didn't need to hide, or pretend anymore. Even with Adam, she had kept a part of herself hidden away…her worry, her fear. But here, with William at her mouth and pussy, she could open wide her heart and soul, finally able to relax and feel safe.

As William licked and sucked at her mouth, the tip of his hard and heavy cock gently moved mere inches in and out. As hot and aroused as she was, electric currents of desire came with each movement they made. As the seconds ticked by, inch by slow inch, she felt William fill her up as she longed for. When he finally penetrated her to the hilt, they both groaned with the bliss of that full feeling only *his* length and thickness seemed to bring.

Josephine could feel William shaking in his effort to hold back his thrusts. He was so gentle it was driving her nuts. She was creaming unbelievably, and so ready for him she felt on the knife-edge of an orgasm. Yet his shallow, gentle thrusts were frustrating her more than relieving the ache she felt deep inside her gut.

As William continued to thrust shallowly within her, Josephine knew she couldn't take much more of this sweet lovemaking. She needed a raw, hard fucking, and she thought William wouldn't object to it if he were driven there himself.

Reluctantly pulling her lips away from his, even just for this moment, she gently bit down on his earlobe, hard enough to get his attention, but not hard enough to hurt.

"I won't break, and I promise you won't hurt the kids. Haven't you fantasized over these last months of fucking me hard and deep? Of pressing yourself into me right to the balls? Of holding me tight against this wall as the heat of the shower pours down on us both, the steam enveloping us, as you ram yourself into me over and over? Please fuck me hard, lover, I promise we'll both enjoy it."

The strangled sound that emanated from William brought an unholy grin of joy to her face. For a moment, she turned her face up to stare into heat and lust-filled, dark blue eyes, and then her lips were being crushed. Closing her eyes in bliss against the force of his passion, Josephine felt William withdraw once from her body, and then slam back into her. He used more force than he previously did, but she could tell he still held himself slightly in check.

The strange mix of rough and gentle spurred her on as nothing else could have. William was not being soft anymore, he gave her the force she desired, yet still restrained himself for the sake of their children. A strange warmth blossomed in her chest. Josephine closed her eyes and tried just to enjoy the moment.

William's pace quickened with every thrust, Josephine moaned as William thrust harder and deeper into her. As she felt her passions rise, choked sounds fell from her mouth. Realizing they were screams she was stifling, she tried to suck in a deep lungful of air.

As her thoughts spun dizzyingly around her, she felt herself rushing up to that magnificent peak of climax. Desperately wanting William to come with her, as she felt the power and waves of pleasure crash and crescendo around her, she reached one slim hand down between their bodies and pinched him very gently in that special place just underneath his balls.

Hearing him utter a hoarse, strangled shout, she felt the colors and vibrations of her own climax rock through her, surrounding her with a safety and bliss she had missed desperately during the last six months. Feeling William's cock thrum and vibrate, and then the feel of his hot seed shoot deep inside her body, Josephine wallowed in their mutual climax.

Over and over William shot into her; deep, hot shots of his cum. He filled her totally with his seed, and she felt the excess slide down her thigh to wash away with the spray of the shower.

Gasping, still feeling the residual tingling and bright colors surrounding her vision, Josephine held on tightly to the only solid thing she knew at this time—the large man in front of her.

As she slowly started floating back to earth, her breaths began to slow from the hurried pants to her more normal deep breaths. Just as her breath returned to normal and got under control, William uttered a bellowing cry as she felt him fumble at the wall.

"Damned hot water service."

Wondering what the hell was wrong, Josephine was about to ask, when she felt the chilling spray of cold water against her rosy, heated flesh.

The hot water had evidently run out. Josephine ducked out of the shower in record time. Picking up one of the fluffy towels she had deliberately left in easy reach, she had to grin at the grumpy, dripping man who followed her out.

Handing him a towel, her smile spread even wider at his disgruntled face. She still felt blissfully sated, despite the water turning cold.

"It lasted a hell of a lot longer than anything else I've had over the last few months."

Blushing as she realized her double entendre, she buried her face quickly in the towel. Glancing up quickly, she had to grin at the smug, utterly male, self-satisfied grin William was shining down on her.

Men!

Chapter Five

ॐ

Snugly wrapped up in one of William's flannel shirts, Josephine watched her lover pull on a pair of cotton briefs for bed. She smiled as she contentedly thought of how sexy but silly he looked in them. The white cotton merely highlighted the lovely deep tan his skin held. The briefs clung almost lovingly to his slim hips, and showed the fine line of his ass to perfection. As she stared at him, his cock began to grow. The tight cotton merely enhanced the perfect bulk of his cock.

William jumped into the bed, snuggled under the covers and dragged her large body closer to his.

"If you don't stop looking at me like that we'll have a repeat of the shower."

"I liked what we did in the shower."

"I know, but I don't want to utterly wear you out. Pregnant women need their rest and sleep. And that's what I'm going to let you do."

Josephine grinned.

"If you want me to sleep the deep sleep of an innocent it's a little late for that, buddy. I'm already fully corrupted by your wicked hands and tongue. And your cock has certainly branded me. But I'm more than happy to share the bed and this lovely large bedspread with you."

William raised an eyebrow.

"Such generosity! I am most humbled, my lady."

He gently, almost hesitantly laid a hand on her huge belly. The reverence and awe with which he moved his hands over their children showed her more clearly than words his love for their babies, his devotion and protectiveness towards them. He closed his eyes for a few moments. Josephine enjoyed the chance she had to study his features. She kept silent, letting him think, or concentrate, or do whatever it was he seemed to want to do.

When she noticed a slight frown puckered his forehead she couldn't keep silent.

"What is it? William, what's wrong?"

* * * * *

William frowned and tried to concentrate. He didn't really know how he did what he did. Usually he merely concentrated and tried to focus on something outside his body. It was something he had always been able to do, so he never needed to question it. When he first met his sister-in-law, Sophie, he was able to scent her and his brother mingled in their baby, and some instinct told him that the child might very well be female.

All the Rutledge children were male, and had been for generations. While he never directly argued the gender of the child with Sophie, he had laughed and joked with his brothers over the strange delusions of a pregnant woman who'd insisted her child was a girl.

He alone had not been totally shocked at the arrival of little Christiana.

Yet this was slightly different. He could definitely feel the two tiny babies living inside his woman, could almost see them. Yet every time he concentrated too deeply on them, he started drowning in Josephine's scent—in their joint scent—surrounding their babies.

There was just something…different.

"…what's wrong?" Josephine's voice finally penetrated his fogged mind.

Removing his hand reluctantly from his little sons, William wrapped himself around Josephine's loving warmth.

"Nothing…I was merely communing with our little boys. As you share a bloodstream with them and can mentally chat to them at any time of the day or night, I have to wait until I have you gloriously naked and under me to do my chatting with them. We'll have to buy some Tchaikovsky and Bach for you to listen to. Apparently sons grow bigger and stronger when their moms listen to those tunes when the fetus is growing."

When Josephine rolled her eyes and turned her back to him, he merely spooned her closer and pressed his half-hard shaft against her delightful ass.

"So how did you know the babies were twins?"

Caught daydreaming about making slow love to Josephine as she fell asleep, William was surprised by the question.

"Ah…sweetheart, this mightn't be the best—"

"Oh please!" she interrupted, "now is the best time. I'm all warm and fuzzy from our passion. Trust me when I say now would be the very best time for you to explain your power to me."

"Power?" William thought for a moment. Josephine didn't appear concerned in the least. Maybe this would be easier than he thought.

"Yes, I presume you have some sort of power. I believe in magic and a lot of that new age crap. Not magic like in the fairy tales, but some psychics are real. I just assumed you had some sort of male version of psychic power."

William nodded against Josephine's back.

"Well, I'm not really sure about that or how it works. Sometimes I can just concentrate and…*understand*…things, see things. It often works a little differently, so I can never predict it. Sometimes when I expect to get something I don't get anything at all. It's rather hard to describe. But there is something I want to tell you…"

142

Pausing to try and gather his foggy, lust-riddled thoughts, William inhaled Josephine's scent. She wriggled adorably, grinding her soft ass against his hardening cock.

"That tickles, William! And don't try to avoid the question. What's up?"

"My brothers and I are all...different...but I'm the only one who seems to have any particular sort of gift like this. But...um..." William's mind wandered as Josephine wriggled in the bed again, obviously trying to find a comfortable position lying down with her expanding belly.

He lowered one of his hands under the flannel shirt. When his warm hand touched her soft, crinkly curls, without thought, his hand started playing. Tunneling through to her engorged clit, he began to stroke.

"William! Don't! Finish what you were saying first! Oooh!"

William couldn't help the grin that covered his face.

Rubbing his finger around and around her engorged clit, he listened to her deepening breaths. When Josephine started canting her hips, to press her clit more demandingly over his stroking fingers, he resumed his talking.

"I don't really know what talent it is, I can simply tell things sometimes. The more I concentrate and focus on it, the hazier it gets."

"You've already said that," Josephine gasped, backing her ass into the cradle of his cock, "but you said that *all* of your brothers were different."

William sighed. Slipping a finger into her wet pussy and thrusting it simultaneously with his stroking finger, he worked to free his shaft with just his free thumb.

"Well, this is going to sound a bit strange, so just trust me, okay?"

Josephine laughed. "You have a finger in my cunt and another one stroking my clit. I'm a minute away from climax, and you think you need to ask me to *trust* you?"

William smiled. His request did seem a bit ridiculous now that he thought of it. His cock was now fully erect and desperate to be inside Josephine, even though they had made love not ten minutes ago. William slowly, carefully began to ease himself into her. Strumming her clit with both wet fingers now, he gritted his teeth in the attempt not to simply plunge inside her. He reminded himself he needed to be careful of the kids.

"*Ohhhh* heavens! That feels wonderful, William!" With Josephine wriggling madly on his impaling shaft, William was finding it harder and harder to concentrate on anything except losing himself in her scent and body. Finally, he was penetrating her right to his balls, and they both gasped to catch their breaths.

Josephine wriggled her delightful ass, incredibly driving him half an inch deeper into her.

"Now talk, buddy. Tell me about this 'difference' you and your brothers have."

Grinning wickedly, nipping at the curve where her neck met her shoulder, William blew gently on her bare neck.

"Well, you see, darling, we're all werewolves. Every month on the full moon, or when the urge comes to us, we change into our wolf form, and run around the National Park howling and scenting prey. My older brother Artemais is the Alpha of the pack, and his daughter Christiana will hopefully follow in his footsteps one day."

Noticing Josephine had stilled, mouth gaping open, trying to turn around to see if he was kidding her or not, William enjoyed this rare moment of stumping her. Easing his rock-hard cock out from her delicious pussy, and then pressing firmly back in, he started a slow, teasing pace for their lovemaking.

"You're kidding me, aren't you, William? That would mean my babies are half werewolf. If this is some sort of joke it's not funny, I'm going to kill you!"

Realizing that he might be upsetting her, William kissed her nape, and kept his pace thrusting.

"I'm not kidding, love. I wouldn't joke about our babies. Just let the thought sit a while, hmm? Relax and let me love you."

Slowly thrusting, building the pace, William gently, reverently, loved his mate. When she peaked again, moments later, crying out and clutching his ass even closer to her body, he felt an overwhelming rush of love and affection for her. Keeping his hands on her hips, not wanting to hurt her belly if he should grab her too tightly in their passion, William continued thrusting through her orgasm, and began building her up once again without pause.

As Josephine threw her head back onto his chest, twisted to look up at his face, she seemed to search his features. He smiled gently down at her, wondering what thoughts were going through her mind.

"You weren't kidding, were you?" she clarified.

William bent down and kissed her nose. "No, love. I wasn't kidding."

Josephine nodded. "You didn't come."

William felt a huge grin cross his face. Increasing the pace of his leisurely thrusts, he felt an insane pride in the fact he could bring Josephine to climax multiple times and barely break a sweat.

"I will this time." He promised.

That time, like he promised, they both cried out in passion, both shuddered in ecstasy, and William felt his seed shoot hot and deep inside his mate, bathing her in his essence.

As he slowly came down from the high, gently returned to earth, he snuggled closer to his mate. She carried his babies, and he knew he would protect her from whatever had happened in Seattle, whatever it was she was running from.

Wrapped tightly around her, William tried to "see" his children, but failed. He smiled slightly as he thought that maybe Fate wanted to surprise him with his sons. As they lay entwined in his big bed together, William decided as he had now shared his secret, it was time for Josephine to share some of her own secrets.

"Josie," he started, hesitantly, kissing her nape again. "Josie, what happened out in Seattle? Why are you running?"

When she gave him no response, he tightened his embrace slightly.

"You can tell me, love, I promise."

When William felt the deep, even breaths puffing from her lungs, he sighed. Ordinarily, the thought of bringing a woman to climax so forcefully and completely that she fell asleep from exhaustion was a calming balm to his male ego. Tonight, however, it was a pity. He really wanted to talk to Josephine about that warrant.

Wrapping her thoroughly in his embrace, determined she would not be able to leave in the morning without a backward glance, William settled himself deeper under the bedspread.

Tomorrow would be soon enough to talk about her problems.

Chapter Six

‿

Josephine woke up with sunlight shining down on her face. As she looked around the unfamiliar room, she felt the warm, secure presence of William's body wrapped tightly around her. Nestling back against his warm body, she blinked and placed her hands protectively over her babies. *Their babies.* She had to keep reminding herself they were no longer merely hers. She would be sharing much of them with William.

For the first time in months, Josephine entertained the fantasy that she and William could raise the children together, happy and secure. Maybe if she simply ignored the problems back in Seattle she could truly try to start over again. Remembering that William was a cop, Josephine winced.

She doubted she could hide forever. While it had been difficult up until now, she had only had herself to hide, to protect. It would be near impossible to hide with two little children. She would have to use her real name on the birth certificates, which would bring Mason and Wells, as well as the Seattle police, crashing down on her head.

Her life was becoming more and more complicated. William stirred next to her, pulling her closer into his embrace, and began to nuzzle her neck. Wriggling, she turned around to face him.

With his hair all mussed by sleep, even straggling all over the pillow and probably knotted down his back, he still stole her breath away with his handsomeness. With his deep blue eyes staring solemnly down at her, she drowned in their sensual depths. In that moment, Josephine forgot all about the time she spent hiding and running, the fear and constant worrying she had faced. Only William, his perfect, broad chest and his smiling face waking up next to hers, mattered.

Josephine crept closer to him, until her large belly rested against his flat stomach. Reaching over, she grabbed both of his large hands in hers, and pressed them gently over her stomach.

"They're more active first thing in the morning. Originally, before I could feel them moving about and kicking me, it was the morning sickness."

Josephine grinned sheepishly at his shocked, worried expression.

"Were you badly sick?"

"Sick enough. It originally was how Adam and I met. I was puking my guts up as he was walking past my room. When he heard the retching and moans through the door he thought someone was messing up the room with a hangover. When he found it was merely a pregnant woman with morning sickness he was really good about it."

Suddenly, there was movement under her skin. Josephine felt the familiar, rolling feeling. She giggled at William's wide eyes and look of utter astonishment.

"He kicked you!"

Josephine rolled her eyes.

"Well, yeah! That's a good sign. Anyway, you can't do anything about it because we can't tell which one it was."

William merely grinned and pressed his hands closer. "Make them do it again."

Sighing in despair, she told William a few of the funnier stories of her pregnancy. The babies kicked a few more times.

After they had been quiet for a couple of minutes, William commented quietly, "We must do this again. I feel as if I've missed so much already. You do want a large family, don't you?"

Josephine paused. She always had wanted three or four children, but she had always envisioned the normal life. A house with the requisite mortgage attached, a husband, a huge traditional white wedding, with a dog and three or four cats and a white picket fence.

Being on the run from the cops, pregnant with twins, no husband, no wedding, and no safe place to decorate for the coming babies was not the situation she had planned.

"I had always planned on three or four. I suppose that's a large family nowadays..." she trailed off, not really wanting to ruin the moment by pointing out her childhood dreams.

William merely nodded and snuggled her closer. Josephine put a hand up onto his chest and tried to think of words to express her question.

"Did you mean what you said last night?"

"Which bit?" he replied easily, not concerned in the least.

Josephine took a deep breath.

"The bit about being a werewolf. I'm sorry, but you must realize how strange and...just plain weird that sounds. It's not that I don't believe you, it's just..."

"So strange, yeah, I get it. At least you're not laughing hysterically at me, that's a start."

When William threw off the comforter and climbed out of bed, Josephine felt her stomach clench.

"William—" She wanted to explain, to justify herself and her doubts. When William merely cut her off with a shake of his head, and started stripping off his shorts, she closed her mouth with a snap of surprise.

What the hell...?

Josephine stared with her mouth agape. She worked her throat, wanted to say something, anything, but she simply stared instead.

William was tall, well over six feet. He was muscled, but in a lean, athletic way. She loved his skin, tanned a deep brown from the sun. His hair, even mussed from sleep, was long, shiny, and gorgeous. His flaccid cock rested against his thigh, Josephine whimsically thought of a sleeping giant. But it was his eyes that drew her, his eyes that she could drown in if she wasn't careful.

Josephine stared at her lover, at the father of her children. A warm, safe feeling rested deep in her chest. This man, she knew without a doubt, would never intentionally hurt her, would care for her children with his last breath, no matter how odd his feelings about her seemed at times. Their children would always be safe and treasured with him.

Suddenly, before her eyes, William shimmered. Josephine blinked, instinctively not believing what her eyes were showing her. Yet even after blinking she still saw it. William's body was…shimmering was the only word she could think of.

In the blink of an eye, William was standing before her one second, shimmering as if he were a cartoon mirage about to disappear, and the next second he was no longer there. An enormously large wolf with a dark brown, shining thick pelt of fur stood beside the bed. The fur was the same shade as William's hair, the deep blue eyes held the same intelligence and knowledge Josephine had come to expect from her William.

Josephine felt her mouth hang open, totally unsure if she believed what was right there before her eyes. Unintentionally, she felt her hands come protectively over her stomach, pressing into her little sons.

This was their daddy.

Josephine took a few deep, calming breaths and still slightly stunned said, "Okay, that is one hell of a party trick."

The huge beast rumbled, in what Josephine instinctively knew was laughter. That man was laughing at her!

"Yeah, yeah, you're a comedian."

Josephine crossed her legs Indian style under the blankets. Unable to help herself, she stared at the truly huge wolf beside her bed, totally unashamed. Never before in her wildest dreams had she imagined werewolves really might exist—no more than she believed in the tooth fairy, vampires or mermaids. She would never have expressed these views to a child of any age, nor would she ever get into arguments with adults who believed, but she *personally* had never thought they truly existed.

Yet watching her lover turn into a wolf in front of her very eyes had a strange effect on her. She felt no fear at all as the wolf pounced onto the large bed. Josephine was feeling a childlike curiosity. Yes, this was a wolf, but it was also William. The eyes that held her gaze were William's. The fur of his thick coat reminded her of his long, soft hair. As the huge beast padded next to her, settled down beside her, she couldn't help herself from stroking his soft fur.

The rich, warm scent of the forest ran through him, the heat from his fur warmed her chilly hands. She stroked him as if he were a gigantic cat. Surprisingly, a rumbling sound emanated from his chest. Josephine swallowed a giggle. He reminded her of a content, tame cat, if one could but ignore the fact he was an enormous wolf with sharp teeth and a cold muzzle.

The idiocy of this thought merely made her snicker more.

"Wow, I think you're going to have some major explaining to do to our sons. I sure as hell won't be able to help them out here. It must be so much fun to run free and wild, to explore as an animal."

She stroked William's soft fur. As the minutes passed, she felt lulled, surrounded by the cozy, safe warmth of his wolf's body. Josephine found herself slightly jealous of William's dual nature, where not ten minutes ago she had been highly skeptical.

When William-the-wolf stirred, she removed her hand. She thought he would jump down from the bed and change back into his human form. When he simply stood on the bed, and with his muzzle started nudging her to lie down, she complied, confused.

As before, the wolf shimmered slightly, then in the blink of an eye, William lay kneeling over her, totally naked. Josephine felt a million questions rise in her mind, yet she lay silent. Something in her knew William wanted, needed to do something.

William lay over her, covering her body with his. Gently, almost reverently, he kissed her, exploring her mouth and lips with his. The kiss was beautiful, yet she could nevertheless feel the leashed fire in him. He stirred her, but this wasn't the ordinary, passionate, heat-filled kiss she had come to expect from her lover.

William moved down her neck, to the juncture between her neck and shoulder. There, he kissed her, but then bit her too. The tiny sting he created wasn't painful, but some sort of heat, maybe some sort of essence or emotion, she whimsically wondered, moved from him to her.

Josephine had no real idea what passed between them, she only knew something did. This kiss had some significance to him, and hence should mean something to her.

Before she could query, or even voice a single word, William moved up from her neck and kissed her lips once more.

For a half second, Josephine wondered if she had dreamed the last ten minutes, wondered if she had finally cracked and gone mad. For just a moment she doubted herself. She questioned if her William had really just turned into a wolf, and if he had kissed and bitten her neck, placed his essence inside her.

When William raised his head and grinned a huge, feral grin, reminding her so strongly of the wolf he was, she smiled back. She hadn't dreamed a thing—she just didn't yet understand the significance of that kiss.

"William, what was that? There was something in that...kiss..."

William laughed and patted her cheek. "Why, Josephine, I just marked you as mine."

With such a bizarre comment as his explanation, Josephine now had more questions arising from that one sentence than the whole previous ten minutes. William cut off her curiosity by climbing off the bed.

"Are you hungry? Sophie, my sister-in-law, was ravenous by this stage of her pregnancy. I swear she ate more than Art and I combined. Drove her nuts. We teased her that the baby had created all this extra room in her she was trying to fill, what with the huge belly she was carrying around. I swear if she could have managed it at the time she would have killed us all."

Josephine climbed out of the bed and shivered. Even with the flannel shirt the morning air was still brisk.

"I don't blame her. A woman is always touchy about her weight. If *you* tried carrying a watermelon around in your stomach for a while maybe you'd understand better. Not only is your body doing strange things to you, but also your hormones are totally out of whack. You suddenly feel not just awkward, but fat, ugly, and unbearably uncomfortable in your own skin. If you or your brothers start teasing *me*, I can promise a swift, painful retribution."

Lost in her search for her underwear, Josephine was surprised when William embraced her from behind.

"I think you're beautiful. Your skin glows, your hair shines. Your body is lush and so feminine it makes me ache with desire and emotion just to look at you. You're still the witty, funny girl I met originally, and I think I'm the luckiest guy alive to have you here."

Kissing her gently, sweetly, Josephine felt herself melting against him. Finally pulling back, she smiled.

"I'm hungry. What do you have to eat? Go cook up a storm while I get dressed."

Licking her lips at the sexy body leaving the room, Josephine tried not to think of the conversation she would soon need to have with William. He undoubtedly wanted all the details of why she had left, why she had returned, and everything else in between.

A part of her brain knew, now that he had shared his secrets with her, he would want her to play fair and share all her secrets with him.

Running her hands through her hair, she took a deep breath and sighed. There was no time like the present, and it wasn't like her to run. She needed to face this all sooner or later, so she might as well bite the bullet finally and make it now.

Pulling on her clothes and running her brush quickly through her hair, five minutes later she was leaving the sanctity of the bedroom. *Breakfast first*, she promised herself, *then* some truthful explanations.

Chapter Seven

✋

William watched Josephine moan in ecstasy as she ate another mouthful of the omelet. The nearly sensual delight she took in eating surprised him. He knew she wasn't putting on an act, as she had eaten three omelets with barely a pause for breath, and now finally she lingered over this one, her fourth.

Finishing the toast, and refilling her glass of juice, he seated himself next to her with a huge grin.

"I never realized you took such sensual delight in eating."

"I never realized you cook like a five-star gourmet chef," she countered.

William grinned and placed a slow, delicate kiss on the nape of her neck. He nibbled at the sensitive spot he'd found the night before.

"If you come back to the house with me, I can whip up even more delicious meals. I leave a lot of my stuff up there simply because I rarely have the time to cook properly down here. I can make you cheesecakes and soufflés so light and delicate they melt like butter on your tongue. I've even perfected my own chocolate soufflé recipe—and I remember how *very* much you love chocolate."

William grinned as Josephine's eyes glazed over at the memory. Back when they had first met, she had simply appeared on his doorstep one night at the stroke of midnight. She had worn a long trench coat, a pair of black stiletto heels so high they almost saw eye to eye. In one hand she held a slim, delicate paintbrush, in the other she held a bottle of what looked like chocolate syrup.

His cock had hardened immediately upon seeing her—he led her inside and the instant the door shut she dropped the coat. She wore a black bustier, laced up the front and back and so tight her already abundant breasts threatened to spill out of the lacy, stretchy material with every breath. The skimpiest pair of matching black lace thong panties and a garter belt holding up the thigh-high stockings completed the wet-dream get-up.

That night had been so long, and so sensual he still got an instant hard-on when he thought of all they had done. He eventually decided to throw out the sheets. The chocolate "war-paint" had been a total pain in the ass to get rid of. Josie had insisted laundry stain remover would get the chocolate out, but he had sprayed so much on all the different spots they left funny markings on the sheets. It had simply been too much hassle for him, and so he threw them away and had bought a new pair of sheets.

They had taken turns tying one another up with a couple of silk ties he found somehow with no blood in his brain—it had all headed much further south and settled there for the night.

Shifting uncomfortably with an incredibly hard cock in the pants he had found in the laundry pile, he wished he hadn't teased her by invoking those memories. Months ago he had bought his own paintbrush and giant man-sized bottle of the hard-to-find chocolate body paint, and he fully intended to return the surprise to Josephine. Right now, however, he needed to talk to her about why she had run from him, and why there was a warrant out for her in Seattle.

"It's a damn pity I never went back to that little shop and bought another bottle of that paint. The shop assistant had assured me one bottle would be plenty for a night—I never realized you were a chocoholic as well—or I'd have bought two bottles."

William grinned as he collected their dishes, rinsed them and put them in the sink.

"Never mind, we have years now. I fully intend to go back to that fantasy. It's been driving me nuts ever since we did it. As you can see, I *still* get hard merely thinking of it. I was about to suggest we get one of my brothers to mind the kids one night so we can rent a motel room and play all night—but on second thought, the more I look at that belly of yours the more I enjoy the thought of having so much more skin to paint as you are right now."

Grinning at her blush, William crossed back over to the small kitchen table and pulled out his chair. Sitting down then drawing Josephine onto his lap, he rested both his hands on her stomach and nuzzled her neck. She squirmed adorably, easing and increasing the ache in his cock simultaneously.

After playing for a moment or two, they both finally settled into a comfortable position.

Josephine sighed. "Now that you've fed and watered me, you're going to make me talk, aren't you?"

William tried to hide his snort of laughter in her back. When Josephine wriggled again, he knew he failed. "That was the general idea. You've really put this off as long as you can, haven't you?"

He reluctantly released her as she crossed back to the counter and made herself a steaming mug of herbal tea. Sipping it, she grimaced, and then sipped again.

"Much like this tea, I hate it—but as I know it's really what's best for the babies, I have to agree with you. Let's go sit on the couch and I'll tell you a little story."

* * * * *

Josephine told her story with no fumbling halts, and for the most part refusing to meet William's eyes. She stared at his half bare bookshelf, out his apartment window to the cold but sunny day outside, at his furniture—anywhere except in his eyes.

She briefly but succinctly told him how she tried to impress her boss by doing the preliminary checks for the yearly audit—and how she found the factory front and then went to her superior.

She heard his indrawn breath at the tale of that last fateful night in Seattle, and glanced at him as he stood to pace restlessly across the room. Quickly averting her eyes, not wanting to see the anger and disgust that would obviously be on his much-loved features, she stared more forcefully out the window and finished her recital.

She had thought through that last night, replayed each and every second, looking for different things she could have done, so many times over the last ten months of hiding that the story flowed easily from her lips. It was old news to her now.

She finished by explaining how she had hidden the original CDs and photocopies of her evidence in a safe place, drained her savings account, packed the small bag of belongings she couldn't live without with her own burnt copies of the CDs, and left town that very night. Her words ground to a halt and she stopped, waited for the recriminations and accusations she fully expected from this honorable police officer.

"That doesn't explain why you left me four months later without saying goodbye and without even giving me, giving *us*, a chance."

For the first time, Josephine looked back at William. He stood rigidly straight and proud, as if expecting her to stand up and hit him. He looked directly at her, daring her to break their eye contact first. Josephine squelched the urge to squirm.

"You're an honorable man, William. You're a cop, first and foremost. Even after the physical relationship we had back then, even though we both tried to keep it as a no-strings-attached affair, we both learned fundamental things about each other. I *know* you always do what's best, what's right. Do you really think I could have told you all this—confessed about this dirty cop—and not expect you to take his side? I was just this piece of ass you were currently screwing. Can you honestly say you'd have taken my side of the story and back me, even against this fellow man in uniform?"

Josephine stood up, getting into the swing of her argument. The fact that William merely stood there, looking at her as if trying to read answers written on her face, just made her angrier.

"Come on! Everyone knows how the worst offense anyone can do is hurt a fellow officer, physically or verbally. What chance did I—a mere glorified gofer—have against the word of the son of the CEO and a police officer? I could have handed them my evidence, sure! And have it conveniently disappear when Petrelli confiscated it late one night. Then it would literally be my word against his. And it doesn't take a rocket scientist to work out who would win in that battle!"

"I would have believed you. I might have searched for both sides of the story, but I certainly wouldn't have handed you over to the police until I knew for certain what you were up against. You were never just a piece of ass to me. I think that's your view on the matter though."

Josephine felt her anger and outrage simmer down at the pain in his quiet statement. Neither of them said anything as William quietly crossed over to the telephone. Pressing one of the speed dial buttons, he turned his back to her.

"Yo, Sammy baby, get your ass out of bed. I have some work for you... Yeah I know it's early, but this is Class A important... Yeah I found her, she was sitting on my doorstep last night... Yeah, yeah, laugh your ass off later, bro. I need you to run as much info as possible on one Petrelli, he's that Seattle cop you mentioned, probably in charge of that warrant, my guess would be... Yeah, I know. Get Dom to start hacking if need be, but be careful, this is serious shit here... Yeah, yeah, I know I owe you, just get on it pronto. We'll be out at the house."

Josephine watched William hang up the phone and turn back to her, his eyes remote.

"You'd better get packed. We have a car trip to make. I'm taking you back to my family's home. That way I can dig a bit deeper into this mess and not worry about you."

Josephine couldn't move, her brain being bombarded with information.

Firstly, she realized she had truly offended William, which was ironic, as it had never been her intention.

Secondly, she now fully understood the depth of her idiotic worries, as she had always known how deeply set his honor was. She should have known that with such an intense personal code of honor that he would have searched the full depth of her side of the story before condemning her — pregnant or not.

Thirdly, the final insult to her intelligence was the knowledge that she loved this man. Seeing the remote, hurt look in his eyes really hit home to her how much she cared about William, how she loved his teasing, his taunting. He wasn't simply a stud in bed, making her body flare to life and driving her wild. She really cared for him, truly deep down. Knowing she had insulted him and hurt him created this awful hole in her chest and stomach.

Knowing her eyes would reflect the huge ramifications of her thoughts, she looked over to catch William's eye, hoping to figure out something intelligent to say.

Before she could even think of a word, William turned from her and stalked into his bedroom.

Josephine sighed. And to think she had wondered if she should berate him for calmly announcing her as his fiancée last night without a word to her. She laughed sadly. Well, there was nothing from that department to worry about now!

Well, it was all too late now. She had never run before in her life, and this fiasco was proof positive that she should never run again! Look at all the problems she had created from running and hiding! She was pregnant and had just mortally insulted the man she loved and the father of her children.

Stuff this! her brain argued. *No more running and no more hiding!* She would apologize, and truly mean it from her heart. If William acted too pigheaded and stubborn to forgive her for her fears and insecurities, then she would just have to work something else out. No longer would Josephine Lomax run *or* hide.

If William thought he was going to take her away from here and hide her in his family home he had another think coming. She wasn't some stupidly naïve teenager, she could help herself and him in some ways. Most importantly of all, she felt an overwhelming urge to prove to William that she did trust him. *First things first* had been a favorite saying of her mother's. Before she could begin to patch the bridge back with William, maybe she should prove a few home truths to him first.

Making up her mind in an instant, swearing curses about the male population in general under her breath, Josephine stomped into the bathroom. She washed her face and patted herself dry. Carefully so she didn't lose her balance, she knelt down onto the floor and opened the cupboard under the sink.

Rummaging around amongst all the assorted paraphernalia that lived and grew under there, she finally found the old paintbrush she had been looking for. Picking it up reverently, she pushed aside the memories it invoked. She also removed the two CDs of burnt information she had hidden with it so many months ago.

Slipping the slim CDs into the enormous pockets of her maternity dress, Josephine checked her reflection one last time and went back into the bedroom where William was still grumpily packing.

Josephine stood silently in the doorway a moment. Even though she had kept one of the copies with her all through her disaster of hiding, Josephine knew she must have trusted William to have left her two spare copies back here with him. Maybe even a tiny part of her had hoped he would find them and come to get her.

Wrinkling her nose in disgust, Josephine hoped to hell that hadn't been the case. She much preferred to think she simply cared about this man and trusted him subconsciously, even when her head had told her to run and hide.

Wondering how to use the CDs to convey these new thoughts and feelings to the big oaf, Josephine bit her lip and pondered her strange situation. She watched William throw jeans and sweaters into a small backpack, along with a clean change of briefs. Josephine felt her now-always volatile emotions start to bubble over.

"Look. I'm sorry, okay? I've been scared for so long now it's like I can't breathe. I didn't want to drag you into this mess. I was scared to tell you and scared not to tell you. I somehow thought this would all blow over really quickly — only it didn't, it just got worse."

Sighing, running a hand through her now messy hair, Josephine searched for words. Magnificent, poetic words eluded her, only the bubbling cauldron of fear, anger and worry burned inside her.

William paused in his packing. He looked at her, but remained silent.

"Once I started running and hiding, everything just snowballed. Running made me look guiltier, and I didn't know any cops I could trust. I didn't have anyone to whom I could give the damned things to and trust not to make them disappear. It's like quicksand; the more I struggled the further I sank. Then I met you, and the last thing I wanted was to drag you into this. If you took my side, you'd have to break your own morals to help me, and I couldn't bear to think you wouldn't believe me and simply turn me in anyway. Either choice seemed bad, so leaving was the perfect solution."

William merely raised an eyebrow at that comment. Determined to get everything out, Josephine continued.

"It took me a while to work out I was pregnant, the stress of hiding and lack of money hasn't been pleasant on my already screwed up metabolism. Once I worked it out, it took me a few months more to screw up the courage to come back here, to you. I do trust you, you moron, or I wouldn't be here. I might be a little stubborn and pigheaded, but I do eventually see the light. Do you really think I'd have come back of my own volition if I thought you were one of the bad guys? I just needed to find my courage."

Taking a deep breath, Josephine angrily wiped at the tears forming in her eyes. She hated weeping women, and was disgusted to find herself wanting nothing more than to run into William's arms and have a good long cry.

"I'm sorry if I hurt or offended you, but I'm here now. I don't want you mad at me. I'm here, I'm sorry, and I don't know if you believe me — but maybe these will help."

Josephine jerkily took a step towards William's big bed. Reaching into her pockets she withdrew the two CDs and threw them gently on his quilt.

Taking a deep breath, praying for the strength not to start crying before she could lock herself in the bathroom, she turned to flee. Dimly, she heard a choked sound come from William, and then she heard his heavier step come quickly across the room. He stood in front of her — blocking her escape.

For a split second she wondered if he would take her arm, drag her outside and down to the precinct. Yet he bent forward and wrapped her in his strong, warm arms in a huge bear hug. No longer could she hold her tears back. With a choked cry that sounded more like a wounded animal than those delicate feminine sniffs her friends used when crying, Josephine bawled her eyes out.

Ten minutes later, she accepted a handkerchief from William and noisily blew her nose. Wiping at her eyes, she fanned her face and grimaced.

"Shit. I hate crying. It's the weakest female thing on earth, and makes me feel like a moron. My forehead gets splotchy, my eyes get bloodshot, and I feel like a dork."

When William laughed, Josephine glared at him.

"Your eyes go a deeper green, almost a cat-like luminescent green, I can't see any splotches, whatever the hell those are, and I think you've been under enough stress and weird hormones for me to excuse it this once."

Kissing her forehead like a father, chucking the CDs into his bag with the rest of his belongings, he resumed his packing with much less anger.

"I wasn't angry at you, nor am I now. I'm angry at the choices you made and at the situation in general. I wish you had confided in me back before you left, but there's no use wishing for things that happened in the past. Thank you for trusting me, for giving me the information. My brothers and I can go over them back at the house. I still want to take you there and keep you safe. We can discuss everything once Samuel and Dominic have more information. Okay?"

Josephine squirmed on the spot, feeling like a three-year-old just caught stealing cookies.

"Uh…I might be able to help you, I really don't want to just be put on a shelf somewhere and told to wait patiently for you 'men' to take care of everything. I'm sorry, but I'm just not that kind of girl. And I left those CDs here—under the sink in your bathroom cupboard. I didn't really know why at the time, it just seemed like a good idea."

"You did? Don't you realize what that signifies?" he queried, smiling even as he ignored her earlier comments.

"Yeah. Sort of. I didn't really know it at the time, but I just worked it out when I saw how truly offended you were. I guess I trusted you on some level even before I left, huh?"

Silently William zipped up his bag, his eyes full of questions and understanding.

Feeling a thousand times lighter and easier, Josephine smiled. Noticing William's unbrushed hair, carelessly tied back in a straggly ponytail, she grabbed his hairbrush and motioned for him to sit down.

"You don't have to—" he said as he sat down on the edge of the bed.

"I know," she interrupted, gently pulling out the knots and smoothing the hair down his back, "but I want to. I think it'll soothe us both a bit. I love your hair, by the way. Can I braid it back? We can play Indian and the Virgin Maiden again. That was a great game."

William half-turned around, looking pointedly at her large belly.

"It might be a bit hard to play Virgin Maiden with that body. How about we play Indian takes a wanton captive?"

Josephine spun out the five minutes it took to brush the knots from his hair into fifteen. The rhythmic, soothing strokes lulled them both into a calmer mood. When William started shifting restlessly, Josephine started the intricate braid, wishing he wasn't in such a rush. Idly, she marveled at how many inches his hair had grown since she left. His hair was now as long as hers, reaching halfway down his back. Licking her lips, she imagined all the things he could do to her as his captive slave.

"I like the wanton captive idea. Hand me a hair tie and we can start."

Securing his hair, she sat down, waiting for the games to begin. When William grabbed her hand and gently pulled her from the bed, she looked questioningly at him. When he picked up her small bag as well as his own in his other hand, she frowned. As he pulled her to the door, opened it and led her out, she laughed in protest.

"Hey! What happened to our Indian game?"

"We're playing it. This Indian is taking you captive back to his house."

Rolling her eyes and giggling, Josephine followed him down to the elevators. She'd have to think of a way to pay him back later, maybe she could pick up some chocolate topping in the supermarket on the way up to his place...

Chapter Eight

As the scenery slowly turned from the outer city and into a more lush landscape, a gorgeous green forest, Josephine was enchanted. The dark green trees grew denser as the miles flitted by, the sky became more and more covered by the overhanging trees, and the weak sun filtered through the overgrowth.

"This is beautiful," she commented for what felt like the millionth time. William laughed.

"Anyone would think you'd never seen a forest before."

"Well, of course I have seen a forest before," she insisted, indignantly, "just not one this dense and beautiful."

Time passed and Josephine felt lulled by the warm car, William's presence, and the soothing motion of the car as it climbed the hills.

The soft touch of William's hand on her arm startled her, and she awoke to find the car parked in front of a huge rambling old home. A large garden, with what looked like freshly planted flowers and herbs, sat out front, and the huge rise of trees behind the house showed they were still on the edges of the large park.

"We're here, honey. Wait a sec and I'll help you out of the door."

Suddenly worried, Josephine grabbed William's arm when he moved to get out of the car.

"Your brothers won't be upset with me, will they? They'll think I'm trying to trap you or something, won't they? Oh my gosh, what do we tell them?"

William smiled and hugged her soothingly. "Nah, they're much more likely to hang shit on me for not following you more carefully and letting you run around for six months pregnant with my kids. We'll tell them the truth, or at least the truth that makes us both look like logical, sane, rational adults."

Inexplicably feeling better, Josephine smiled and sat back.

"Oh, well, that's okay then."

Laughing at his mock frown, Josephine shuffled back against the door when William growled and moved forward to kiss her. She reached up to tug his long braid as he crowded closer to her. Drowning in his kiss, feeling the car heat up by degrees as his tongue entered her mouth and started tangling with her own, Josephine bolted upright when she heard a male shout "Hey!" suddenly.

"Oh!" she gasped, looking around nervously.

William stroked her cheek, muttering a curse.

"It's only Art, my elder brother. He has the world's *worst* sense of timing, and it's not improving now he's a daddy. You'd think we were teenagers caught necking outside our dad's front door!"

Sighing at his disgust, Josephine tried to hide her smile as William got out of the car and came around to her side. Despite her hatred of feeling delicate and helpless, she did feel better knowing at least he wouldn't let her fall flat on her face in front of his brother.

Accepting his helping hand, she awkwardly climbed down, cursing her lack of grace. She could see the first impression she would give—hugely pregnant after running for six months. She sighed in dismay. This wouldn't be easy.

A tall man, though not as tall as William, with the same bedroom blue eyes and dark brown hair, though cut far shorter than William's, approached them and slapped William on the back.

"Hey there, Wills, you've been gone for a while. Sophie was starting to talk about dragging you back here herself…"

"William!"

Before the man could finish or introduce himself, a blonde woman with a tiny baby held protectively in her arms came rushing out of the house. Rushing down the few stairs from the front porch, she ground to a halt, handed the baby over to her husband, and threw herself in William's arms.

Josephine was too surprised at this energetic woman to feel even a spark of jealousy over her familiarity with her William. She recalled William talking about his sister-in-law, Sophie, and guessed this was she. Blinking as the woman simultaneously pulled herself out of the hug and turned to her, she felt the full force of this woman's smile.

"You must be Josephine. I am *so* glad William finally found you. He's been moping around here for *months* and then suddenly after Christiana was born, he upped and left without a word to anyone, and hasn't been back since. It's only been a little while, but I have become so used to this place being overrun with the Rutledge men, it seemed so strange with some of them missing!"

Josephine felt a slender arm wrap around her shoulders. Next thing she knew Sophie was helping her up the stairs and into the house, still talking a mile a minute.

"I know these stairs are a pain in the ass when you're so burdened already, but the back door has no stairs, so you can just use that later. William's rooms are closer to the back of the house anyway. You must be what? Seven and a half months along?"

Josephine smiled.

"Just on six months, actually. But they're twin boys."

"Twins!" Artemais crowed. "You just had to beat me, bro, didn't you?"

Sophie shot a glance at him and stuck her tongue out at him.

"These men are disgraceful. Just wait until you meet Dominic and Samuel at lunch! They're wonderful, but they have no concept of womanly independence. No driving alone. No walking alone. No *shopping* alone! Really! I figure if now that you're here we can gang up on them and do things together and try to curb some of their protective instincts."

"Uh. Well…" Josephine trailed off as she entered into a large, sunny kitchen. She had no idea how long she would be staying, or even if she would be staying. Looking to William for help, he merely smiled at her in that secret way he had.

"I think we should be able to get some girl time in. But I'm not really sure how long I'll be here."

Sophie glanced from her to William.

"Not sure? William! If you dare tell me you haven't proposed I'll…I'll…" spluttering in her outrage, she calmed down when Artemais handed the tiny baby back to her. It didn't stop her spluttering, but she cradled the infant protectively in her arms, calming her in some measure.

"Now Soph, I'm sure William is doing the right thing in his own time." Shooting a hard stare at his brother, he raised his eyebrow. "But for now, I bet poor Josephine needs a bit of a nap, hmm? William can show you his rooms. You're more than welcome to stay for as long as you like. My brothers and I own this huge place jointly, and there's more than enough room for you and the kids when they arrive. Christiana will probably love the company by that time."

Feeling William come up beside her and wrap a warm arm around her shoulders, Josephine smiled, enjoying the easy, friendly relationship these adults seemed to share.

"Thank you, Art. I'm not sure yet what my…uh…our plans are, but I really do appreciate the offer. I would love to settle in and have a bit of a walk around outside. I didn't realize the forest was literally in your backyard."

"No problem. And just take William or myself with you when you wander. Sophie is useless, even after all these months she *still* gets lost more than a hundred feet outside the house, don't you, dear?"

Sophie blushed, even though Josephine knew the tone was light and teasing.

"Don't you dare embarrass me in front of my new friend. I can tell Josephine and I will be able to stand strong against you men. Go on and settle yourself, Josie. We can chat later. As for you," she glared at William, "we will talk much sooner."

William merely grinned at her and bowed in a surprisingly courtly manner.

"I am always at your disposal, sister dear. You merely need to pound on my door, as you always do."

Josephine couldn't help the huge smile that spread across her face. She could tell the teasing and jeering that would continue over dinner when the other two brothers arrived would indeed prove interesting.

Smiling at Sophie, Josephine let herself be led around the side hall and into one wing of the house. Even though it wasn't far at all from the kitchen, the old winding corridors gave the feeling of being far removed from the main dining area. William opened a door and led her through the connecting rooms into what surely was his part of the expansive old house.

William threw his small overnight bag onto a couch and placed her larger bag by the closet door. Dragging her into his arms, he embraced her fiercely and kissed her long and hard. Feeling a bit stunned when he finally pulled away, she tried to gather her scattered wits.

"Welcome home, Josephine."

Chapter Nine

ℭ

Blinking rapidly, trying to dispel the fog created by William's passion, Josephine felt the words sink in her stomach. Was this really her home? If she stayed here, then Artemais or Sophie would eventually wear William down and he would propose. And much as she'd love to get married and raise her babies here on the edge of the most beautiful forest she had ever seen, he would be marrying her for all the wrong reasons. She wanted to be married for herself, because her man simply couldn't live without her, not because she was carrying his children or his family had backed him into a corner.

Josephine would love nothing more than to have William declare his eternal love and devotion—both to her and their children—but she refused to be forced or bullied into a marriage simply because she was pregnant. She deserved more. Her babies deserved more.

Looking around the rooms, wondering how long she should stay, she mentally debated the wisdom of sharing her thoughts.

"I know that look," William growled. "Josie, tell me you aren't thinking of leaving again!"

Josephine blushed. William had always had a fair grasp on her emotions, now he seemed even more attuned to her.

"Well," she hedged, "I'm not going to stick around if you're going to be forced to propose to me. Think of how embarrassed you'll be when I constantly turn you down!"

"Why would you turn me down, love?"

Allowing him to lead her carefully over to the window seat, Josephine sat down and tried not to lean into the

171

comforting warmth of William's body as he sat down next to her.

"Because I deserve more than to be married simply because I'm pregnant and it's expected of you."

William opened his mouth to protest, but Josephine cut in.

"No, William, think about it. Marriage hadn't really crossed your mind before Sophie brought it up. So you can save us both a stack of embarrassment and not propose. My answer will be no, so let's just say you did and move on, okay?"

William narrowed his eyes and stared at her thoughtfully.

"Does this have anything to do with my being a werewolf?"

Josephine looked confused. "No. Why? Should it?"

William looked at her a moment longer, then stood up, holding out his hand.

"I really don't want to argue. Let's go take a walk in the forest before dinner. I can show you some of my favorite spots. We'll take it slow and easy so you don't tire out."

Agreeing readily — there was no point in saying anything more on the subject of marriage — Josephine changed into a clean pair of jeans and walking shoes and followed William outside.

William led her around their backyard, taking his time and slowly pointing out the herb garden their mother had planted many years ago and that he and his brothers had kept weed-free and fertile in her memory. The backyard itself was quite large, with a meandering path that seemed to increase its size, not decrease it.

When they finally reached the gate in the back fence, William opened it and let her look at the dense forest beyond. When she stepped forwards, expecting to wander a short distance into the forest, William stood still and gently held her hand back.

"It's the National Park out there. I really wish you and Sophie didn't wander alone out there. Sophie, lovely girl that she is, has no sense of direction. She'll get you lost faster than you'll ever realize. I hesitate to forbid you to do anything…"

Josephine glared at him, a dangerous glint in her eye. She hoped William understood that she wouldn't take orders very well at all.

"…but I really want you to think hard about your own safety, and the safety of our children before you go wandering around without me or one of my brothers. Okay?"

Josephine saw the genuine concern in William's eyes, and smiled. He really wasn't trying to play Lord of the Manor, but make her realize how serious the situation could be.

She nodded. "Okay, William. I won't go wandering out of the backyard without you or one of your siblings."

William hugged her close and kissed her tenderly. "Thank you, sweetheart. That means a lot to me. Let's head back—I bet you're hungry."

Josephine grinned as her stomach rumbled.

"Oh boy, am I hungry. Feeding your sons is proving to be my ultimate downfall. Is Art a decent cook?"

William laughed. "He wasn't always, but with Sophie eating him out of house and home while pregnant, he learned a number of important lessons—like when to *not* wake up a sleeping pregnant woman, how to cook a decent, hearty meal, and that the pregnant wife is *always* right."

Sobering up mid-laugh at the word "wife", Josephine looked away.

"Hey," William caught her chin and tilted her face to look directly into his. "You *will* marry me, love. You're carrying my kids and you've come to me for help and protection. Whether you realize it or not, you trust me and you care for me."

"It's not a matter of what *I* feel for you. I know those feelings. It's more I don't want you to feel trapped, that you *have* to marry me."

William shook his head. "Arguing logic with pregnant women is insane. Art warned me, but I didn't listen to him. Talk to Sophie if you don't believe me, Josephine. She knows better than anyone else how much I care for you, how much I worried for you these last few months." Kissing her gently, chastely, he drew back before Josephine felt herself falling too deeply under his spell. She was both relieved and frustrated as he pulled back.

"Come on, let's go inside," he said, taking her hand again.

Josephine trailed a step behind her lover, mulling over his words. As she entered the massive house, she heard raucous male laughter from within the kitchen area. William swore under his breath and, after squeezing her hand a moment, hurried in that direction.

Happy for the brief moment to catch her breath and steel her courage, she too followed the sound of laughter and cheerful male jeering.

"So your ladylove is pregnant with *twins*?" she heard a man's voice crow. "Wills, you nearly lost your stomach watching Sophie give birth, how will you cope with watching *two* of them pop out?"

Josephine felt herself bristle and start to storm into the kitchen to defend her love. She felt a delicate hand hold her arm back. Turning, she saw Sophie grinning behind her.

"Hang on a sec, let me give you the background on these guys first. That's Dominic teasing William. You might want to know he was standing next to William on the far wall, about to toss his cookies in the birthing room. He was as bad, if not worse, than William." Josephine felt a smile cross her face as Sophie winked cheekily at her. "No point in simply blowing your top. Might as well know the inside information."

"Thanks," Josephine grinned and stomped into the kitchen.

"The way I hear it, *you* must be Dominic."

Her loud comment, easily heard over the male laughter and ribbing, had the exact effect she desired. The four brothers all stopped their laughter and looked slightly embarrassed caught jeering each other about her impending labor.

Josephine glared at the sexy man with shoulder-length hair the same dark brown they all wore. Beautiful blue eyes turned to her, full of laughter and mischief and she squashed the impulse to forgive him his teasing.

"The way I hear Sophie's labor went—you weren't in much better shape. Standing against the wall for support, right next to William, looking ready to empty your own stomach."

Raising an eyebrow at the shocked expression on all four male faces, she wondered if she had hurt their male pride more than she bargained for. Remembering William's casual arrogance, she instantly dismissed the stupid notion. When first Artemais, and then Samuel held their stomachs and started laughing so hard tears fell from their eyes, she grinned mischievously at Dominic.

Looking from one brother to the other, and then focusing on her, Dominic crossed the room. He enveloped her in a huge hug, and kissed her on the cheek.

"One thing you can say about William, he has impeccable taste in women. Welcome to the family, little Josephine. Man," he commented, pulling back to get a proper look at her belly, "I'm glad I was warned they were twins, otherwise I'd be worried you were carrying a giant in there."

"That's no way to talk to my woman, Dom! Apologize right now!" William growled from the doorway.

Josephine smiled and patted Dominic on the cheek. Turning to William, she smiled. "That's okay, he didn't mean it in a rude sense, I understand. But I am *starving*. When's lunch?"

Both Dominic and William looked at the still hysterically laughing Art and Samuel.

"I think we can whip something up. What do you say, bro?"

"No problem," William responded easily. "Josephine, take a seat. How would you like some pasta?"

Letting herself get helped to a seat at the kitchen table, Josephine smiled at her lover.

"Pasta sounds just fine thanks. How about a salad as well?"

Chapter Ten

ઐ

By unspoken agreement, there was no mention during the huge meal of Josephine and her plight, or her running away. Dominic and William cooked up enough al dente ravioli and bolognaise sauce to feed an army. Between the four large men, Josephine's enormous appetite, and Sophie grabbing her own bowlful, there wasn't a lot left over.

After a heated argument on the propriety of largely pregnant women doing so many dishes, the six adults settled down in easy chairs, Josephine being pulled into William's lap.

"So," Art started, "tell us what's been going on. I have bits and pieces of the story from Sophie, but she said much of it was in confidence between the two of you, so I'm still hazy on the details."

Josephine, feeling sleepy from the sensation of a full belly and the comforting warmth of William's embrace, nudged him.

"It's okay, you tell them. I'll sit here and interrupt you every now and then."

Quickly and succinctly, William explained the story. When he mentioned the burnt CDs, both Art and Samuel instantly pounced.

"CDs? Where are they?" they asked, practically in unison. William smiled up at a drowsy Josephine.

"Oh, I hid them down in William's apartment a couple of mornings before I originally left. They were...uh...in the back of his cupboard under the bathroom sink, but I collected them and handed them over to him before we left to come out here. He put them in his backpack—I'll grab them—do you have a laptop you can set them up on?"

Dominic and Artemais instantly started planning their method of attack as Samuel rushed out, presumably to get the laptop. Josephine hid a smile at how William simply sat back, thinking. As she stood up out of the chair to go and collect the CDs, she noticed his strange expression. He had finally realized one of the significant actions of where she had hidden them.

"Isn't that where we hid...?" he quietly started, then trailed off. She smiled.

"Well, yeah. It seemed fitting somehow. I knew eventually you'd clean up under there and come across them, and I knew they'd be safe there and in your care when you found them."

The morning after what Josephine privately thought of as their chocolate sauce night, she and William had reverently placed the then-destroyed paintbrush in the back of the cupboard. William had insisted it be their secret, as either one of them could get it the next time they were in the mood for a little body painting.

Josephine had been looking for months for a safe hiding place for the information. She decided to keep the printouts with her, but she worried about losing the CDs. She felt a sense of unreality at how everything turned out all right, even though she hadn't always been sure what was going on.

Josephine looked down at William. For a minute, she wished she could read minds — his in particular. William's eyes were scanning her face, but she couldn't read any of the thoughts going on behind his eyes. She simply looked back at him.

William looked at her for a minute longer, then returned to the main conversation as Josephine headed toward William's rooms.

Quickly grabbing the CDs from his backpack, she hurried back to the main living room. Samuel had already set up the thin, top-of-the-line laptop, which Dominic was typing furiously on, brow furrowed in concentration. Samuel was searching the carry-case the laptop had evidently been removed from, griping about the two cheap-ass CDs he had found inside it, which Dominic would have to use to copy the information onto. Art and William were chatting in the far corner, too far away for Josephine to overhear what they were talking about, but by the serious look on their faces she bet it was related to her plight.

Shaking her head, she handed the CDs over to Dominic. "They're just CDs, guys, not the crown jewels or anything."

"We'll see, Josie, we'll see," Dominic muttered as he slid the first disk into his laptop.

Josephine stood behind him, watching the neatly ordered accounting books appear on the screen.

She waited patiently as Dominic hastily scrolled down them, obviously just skimming them, until she pointed out the relevant files.

"There, that's the factory."

As Dominic opened the relevant folder, the three brothers crowded around the small laptop. William gently pried her away from the group.

"This might take a while, love. Why don't you go up and keep Sophie and Christiana company? You can girl-chat while we mull and nitpick down here. It'll be very slow and boring with these guys, trust me."

Josephine sighed. "Well, I do feel like a quick nap, after all that traveling and that delicious food. Just wake me up in an hour or so, okay?"

William simply smiled, and kissed her softly. When he pulled away, Josephine smiled.

"What kind of kiss was that?"

He leaned forward to whisper in her ear. "That was a my-brothers-are-watching-us-like-hawks-even-if-they-don't-seem-to-be kind of kiss. I promise to make up for it later tonight, when we're alone in our rooms."

Josephine smiled mischievously. "You could come up and have a nap with me, you know."

William groaned in her ear.

"Don't tempt me, love. You have no idea what sort of reaction that will create down here though. It took us *months* to stop teasing Art when he'd take a nap with Sophie. Particularly when there's such important work down here to do I'd simply never live it down. Go on up and I'll join you as soon as we're done. Just have a quick nap and I'll think of a novel way to wake you, hmm?"

Josephine smiled, kissed him once more and said her goodbyes to the other brothers.

In William's rooms, she had a quick shower, getting in and out as fast as possible as even this different shower gave her heated memories of William's shower in his apartment.

Changing into super-baggy sweats, she crawled into William's huge bed, snuggled down under the covers and was soon deeply asleep.

Chapter Eleven

ဢ

Tony Petrelli drove up to the tiny village on the outskirts of the National Park. It was just after noon, and he was weary and hungry from all the traveling he had done in the last few weeks.

That stupid broad had caused him far more hassles than he could ever have envisioned. At least his contacts were all still blissfully unaware of the potential problems.

One of his snitches had finally found the owner of a bar complaining far and wide of his heavily pregnant waitress working so close to her due date, apparently desperate for the money. The story itself was not unusual; it was the shiftiness and anxiety that surrounded the girl and her similar name that had drawn Petrelli's instincts.

Discrete inquiries and an exchange of money passing hands had netted him all her current details. As he headed over to investigate personally, the tail he had placed on her had kept him informed as she headed back across the state of Montana and apparently into the arms of a fellow cop.

Petrelli could have smiled with how she appeared to be making life so easy for him. He could show his badge, sling a little BS and have her "safely" under his jurisdiction hopefully by the end of the day. A little accident on the long car ride back to Seattle and his worries would be over.

Smiling to himself at how easy everything was panning out to be, he parked just outside the only small hotel in the tiny village. William Rutledge's next door neighbor, a friendly old lady, had been only too eager to divulge all her gossip when his badge had been flashed. Her directions were clear and concise. Petrelli felt that the fact everything fell so neatly into place could only be a sign of good things to come.

Booking himself a room, he asked the old man behind the registration desk where the best place for a hot meal would be. The broad might be important, but at the moment a hot meal and a quick nap seemed far more urgent. And anyway, with everything being sewn up so neatly, who the hell needed to rush?

"Only one place to eat around here, and that's the café. They can serve you something hot if you'd like. Simple fare, but certainly tasty."

Thanking the man, he headed out to collect his meal.

He found the café to be much like the rest of the village, small, but clean and well run. Settling for toasted sandwiches, which were easy to bring back to the hotel, he chatted to the young waitress, who introduced herself as Rita.

Delicately phrasing his questions, he found that William Rutledge did indeed live in a large house just a short drive up from the village. He smiled politely and thanked Rita for both the information and the bag of steaming sandwiches she placed before him.

Back in his hotel room, he sat on his clean bed to eat the simple lunch in his sparse room.

Having driven for the best part of thirty-six hours straight, he knew a quick nap was in order before heading out to talk to William Rutledge. Knowing how most cops thought and trusted their fellow officers, Tony had no worries about being able to convince William that the bitch Josephine had lied to him, whatever farfetched story she had conned him with.

He smiled meanly about how nice it would be to finally see her face, watch all her carefully naïve plans fall to pieces around her. His gut knew the whole pregnancy thing was a sham designed to garner sympathy and maybe even throw him off the scent. How stupid could a woman really be?

After setting the alarm clock for three hours hence, he lay down on the bed and plotted his strategy one last time.

It should be easy convincing the country hick that a city girl had lied to him, pulling the wool over his eyes. It was doubtful that she had confessed anything even remotely close to the truth. There was a warrant out for her detainment and arrest; she was implicated in drug pushing and possible smuggling. Tony had the law behind him and proof of the facts he would be impressing on Rutledge.

He had brought a copy of the warrant with him — and that alone should be enough to convince a country hick with no knowledge of the story behind the slut's dealings. Simply showing the warrant and his badge would probably be enough to have Rutledge handing over the broad's current hiding place and washing his hands of the whole scenario, thinking he was doing the right thing — which indeed he was.

Laying back and closing his eyes, Tony smiled. After the "accident" he could continue with his plans for the factory, he'd just be more subtle this time and wipe the records that moron Jonathon hadn't thought of. Everything was falling nicely into place.

Compared to his dealings with mobsters, hardened criminals, and hyped-up junkies, dealing with a stupid female accountant, and a country cop was a cakewalk.

This would be like taking candy from a baby.

* * * * *

Josephine woke up to a curiously quiet house. The afternoon sun shone brightly through the open curtains and into the masculine bedroom.

Josephine smiled sleepily. If she were going to stay here, she would definitely have to add a few touches of her own. A new bookcase for one thing, maybe a few plump cushions in the window seat for another.

Elizabeth Lapthorne

Rubbing her eyes, she turned over and glanced at the clock. 3:04 p.m., it read.

Blinking, she sat up and looked again. Why hadn't William woken her up, or joined her? Getting out of bed and changing back into her maternity dress, Josephine put on her socks and shoes and waddled out of William's rooms, stretching her aching muscles.

The house was weirdly quiet—surely the guys were still looking at that damned information and arguing over what they wanted to do?

Josephine found Sophie in the kitchen, making a pot of tea.

"Where are they?"

Sophie made a face and grabbed two mugs from the cupboard. "They're off down in the village, playing their manly games."

"Manly games?" Josephine queries, confused.

"Yeah, have a seat, the dandelion and chamomile tea is nearly ready."

Josephine made a face. She *hated* herbal tea, but the doctor had cautioned her against regular tea and any coffee. Sophie caught a look on her face and laughed.

"You get used to it, trust me. I hated the stuff all throughout my pregnancy with Christiana, but Artemais wouldn't let me drink anything else. He made the guys hide their coffee and real tea in their bedrooms, so I wouldn't steal some of it. The only thing you'll find in here is the herbal stuff...and now I can't seem to drink anything but it. Maybe you can be a good influence over me and at least get me back onto Earl Grey."

Josephine sat down as Sophie placed a steaming mug full of weak-yellow filled tea in front of her.

"Oh trust me, the instant these boys pop out I'll be bringing in only the best. I don't know how people can think drinking flowers can be good for us. It tastes disgusting."

Sophie laughed as they sipped their tea.

"So, why have the boys left us alone up here, when they get to go down and have all the fun?"

"Well," Sophie smiled, "both you and Christiana were down for your naps. William and Artemais quite rightly didn't want me coming with them and leaving the two of you alone. Now that you're up, Little Miss should be up shortly, and we can go down into the village. There's a shop down there I simply *must* introduce you to, and then we can join the boys. I bet they're in the café, drinking a beer and 'plotting their strategy'."

Both Josephine and Sophie laughed at the mocking tone she used.

"Ah well," Josephine finally hiccupped out when their giggles had died down, "I suppose the only strategy that can really work is I'll have to head back over to Seattle and trust the cops with everything. I'll file a report and with luck that will be the end of my involvement. I really should have done that from the start, but it was a rather scary thought doing it alone, particularly when I really didn't think I could trust the cops."

Sophie reached over and took her hand.

"That's okay, just think of it like this. If you hadn't run, you'd never have met William, and you certainly wouldn't be enormously pregnant with twins and a ready-made family, would you?"

Josephine smiled. "No, that's true."

"So," Sophie smiled and got up. Crossing over to the fridge, she pulled out an extra-large tub of yogurt. She grimaced in sympathy when Josephine made a disgusted face at the tub. "Tell me all about the pregnancy. I suffered from the *worst* case of afternoon sickness in the history of womankind…"

She trailed off as a loud, screeching wail cut through the house.

"Ah, damn." Hastily replacing the tub of yogurt in the fridge, Sophie slammed it shut again. "That's Little Miss Princess now, but at least we can feed and change her and be on our way. Wait until you see this place, it has the most delicious lingerie and whoo-boy, the toys..."

As Josephine followed Sophie into the baby's room, she frowned.

"Toys? The twins aren't even born yet; I might wait a while to get them some toys."

Sophie turned back to grin hugely at her. "No dear. Not toys for the babies, *adult* toys."

Josephine's eyes lit up. "Oh, *perfect*! Do you know if they have any paintbrushes?"

* * * * *

Tony Petrelli pulled on his coat and picked up the keys to his room. Heading down to the registration desk again, he rang the bell on the desk.

The same old man who had signed him in earlier came forward from the back room where soaps blared from an ancient TV.

"Oh, it's you," the man started. "I saw William just a little while ago. He's in the café down the road."

"Thank you," he replied easily, glad he wouldn't need to bring out his identification. He had decided while dressing that if it became necessary, he would bring out his badge and cop ID, to smooth the way, but the less people he needed to inform, the better.

Tony trotted down the street to where the grocery store, gas station, and handful of small shops were scattered around a bar and a café. Slowing down to a leisurely stroll, he casually entered the small café.

The bell above the door rang out, and he managed to keep from flinching at the declaration of his entry. Quickly glancing about, Tony saw that no one paid him any mind. The café was almost empty at this mid-afternoon hour. The smell of cooking onions and roasting meat emanated from the kitchen, a young waitress sat at the counter, snapping gum and reading what looked to be a girl's magazine.

The only customers were four men crowded around one tiny table, solemnly talking. Knowing that one of these men must be William, Tony let his eyes wander over all four of them quickly, but carefully.

That casual glance was enough for him to realize that these men were related. Each had the same colored hair, and roughly the same build. With similar facial structures, Tony figured they were possibly cousins, or more likely, siblings. Used to such monkey wrenches being thrown his way, Tony walked up to the waitress with barely a pause in his step.

"A coffee and a copy of your newspaper, thanks, love," he casually said, laying down a bill on the counter. Picking up the paper the waitress nodded at, he headed over to a table a few yards back from the brothers and waited for his coffee.

Opening his paper and pretending to study it intently, he tried to hear as much of the conversation as possible. Lifting his glance to the waitress every moment or so, Tony felt his gut clench when he noticed two shiny CDs on the table between the men.

Now eavesdropping in earnest, he started when the waitress brought over his mug of coffee.

"Like to order?" she queried.

"Not just yet, thanks, ma'am. I'll just drink this up and order afterwards. Thank you."

Relieved when she nodded, bored and not really paying attention, he watched her walk back towards the counter. Tony snapped his paper, pretending to read it and resumed his eavesdropping on the men's conversation.

* * * * *

"Yeah, I really do think there's enough evidence here, guys. These records clearly show how that factory was being used to siphon off very small amounts of money from the company—over at least the last year, and most likely far more than that. Surely a full audit would reveal the true extent of everything?"

William looked at his brothers across the table, feeling oddly restless. He had that itching sensation he sometimes felt. He knew the man seated behind them was paying attention to what they all said, but simple curiosity wasn't a sin, and certainly wasn't criminal.

No, it was something else—something to do with Josephine. He could almost *feel* her getting up to mischief, and with her in Sophie's company, he could practically place bets on their getting into trouble together.

He kept on glancing at Art, who seemed blissfully unaware of his growing unease. Either Art knew what was going on—or he was completely ignorant of the trouble brewing.

Given that Art had never showed indications of his own...*awareness*...William felt certain that it was only he who had this itching, bizarre feeling of impending doom.

Hearing his name, he jolted back to the conversation. "Uhh..."

Dominic snorted. "Daydreaming again, bro? You've got it so bad. Can I be best man this time?"

Frowning, William nodded, gesturing for them to go over their conversation once again.

"We were talking about you going back to Seattle with Josephine, escorting her around the cop shops over there. Make sure she doesn't get shafted, or worse, that these CDs go missing. We can keep copies over here—just as a precaution—but we really think you should watch over her over there. You can also make sure she doesn't stay too long, so the kids can be born out here."

"Yeah, plus we really should let the locals laugh at Wills doing those dumb-ass Lamaze classes, like they snickered around Art every time he tried to buy sardines and milk, or whatever Sophie was craving that day."

The brothers laughed and started ribbing each other. Artemais raised an eyebrow, rising above the mockery of his brothers.

"I'll have you know we won the internal award of 'Most Breathy' in those damn classes. Not that it was a lick of help in the damn birthing room. Personally, I think it'd be much more useful learning how to calm rabid animals and prevent serious bodily harm from the way Sophie acted that day. And it's not like you have much time to prepare, bro. You have what? Three months at most before Josephine pops."

William laughed and listened with only half an ear to his brother's teasing. He simply couldn't shake the feeling of gloom that was overtaking him more every second.

* * * * *

Damn, damn, damn, damn.

The bitch really was pregnant? How she had convinced the stupid hick it was *his*, Petrelli would never understand. He would never be able to get his head around why men believed everything lying, conniving women such as her fed them. He tried not to swear aloud and pound the table in frustration. He needed to revise his plans, immediately.

Tony stared at the CDs. So close, less than three feet away, yet they might as well be on the other end of the world.

Tony's brain whirled. Both the CDs, and the bitch were here in this tiny village. One was right in front of him, taunting him with its nearness. All he needed was a bluff strong enough and he could grab them and run before anyone could do anything.

The CDs he could deal with, by the sounds of things the country bumpkins hadn't bothered to copy them just yet. It was the woman who seemed to be the problem. He needed to get rid of her. He should never have left a job so important to that idiot Jonathon. Stupid rich boy, he botched everything he touched.

All he needed to do was menace the brothers with his gun, steal the CDs and find where they were hiding the bitch. He was a cop and a thug, he reminded himself. He could bluff his way through this.

*   *   *   *   *

Laughing and joking, the brothers decided their manly retreat had stretched on long enough.

"Come on, guys, let's head back before Sophie and Josephine redecorate the house in green and gold or something from boredom."

William felt a tiny bit of his itchiness fade. Maybe he was simply missing Josie. Reaching for his wallet to help pay the food bill, he noticed Art do a double-take with his glance outside the café.

"What the…?"

Following Art's line of sight, William felt his heart still in pure fear. Both Josephine and Sophie were coming down the street, swinging shopping bags and brown paper-wrapped packages, chatting and laughing together in the weak sunlight.

It was neither the thought of the purchases she had made, nor the fact they were here in town that had fear pumping through his veins. It was some primal instinct, some gut-level reaction that screamed at him that Josephine shouldn't be here.

William couldn't say what made him hone in on this, but his itchy instinct that had been giving him grief for the last half-hour kicked into full-fledged fear. Something definitely wasn't as it should be, and he had to get Josie out of here as quickly as possible. Both his years as a cop relying on his instincts as well as his years as an intuitive male all kicked into gear. He couldn't explain it, but if he acted quickly enough, hopefully whatever was going wrong could be diverted.

At Artemais' stormy countenance and William's frozen shock, both Dominic and Samuel finally noticed something had caught their attention.

Before anyone could say or query anything, the man sitting behind their table rose and came forward, his hand held menacingly inside his large leather jacket.

"I'll take those CDs off your hands, thanks very much. And then you can tell me where that bitch Lomax is."

William felt the fear and adrenaline pump through his body. Coiled and poised for a fight, he felt the thin hairs on the nape of his neck stand up in anger. The blood and adrenaline pumping through him made him shake, his body querying whether to stay calm or beat this man to a bloody pulp.

Never had he felt such a fierce reaction to anything. A still sane part of his brain tried to babble caution. He had never seen this man, didn't even know who he was, yet simply because he had called Josephine a bitch, he felt justified in beating the shit out of him. William still wasn't certain if this man was the threat to Josephine, or if he was merely a diversion. Either way, William could barely think for all the adrenaline pumping through his system.

William vaguely registered both Art and Samuel flanking him, gently holding his arms, cautioning him. He vibrated with the need to rip and tear at this man who insulted his mate.

Artemais turned to face the strange man. In a very low, very possessive voice that William barely recognized, he growled, "This is my town, buddy, and my brother here is the law. I would seriously recommend you cut your losses and simply disappear, without the girl or the information."

"Don't be ridiculous," the angry man snapped, taking another step towards the table. William registered if the man had the guts he could reach forward and grab at the thin CDs, lying in the middle of the small table.

"If those records become public I am totally ruined. Not only will I have every Seattle cop actively hunting me to clear their good name," he sneered, "but I'll also have half the Seattle mob gunning for me for compromising one of their most lucrative exchange ports. The only thing other than these annoying disks I need is the damn Lomax woman. She could blab and ruin everything. *Tell me where she is.*"

William felt his heart stop as the bell above the door rang, signifying their time had run out. He felt time slow down, and his heart rate speed up so fast he worried he'd disgrace himself and pass out.

From the corner of his eye he saw Josephine enter the small café, head thrown back and eyes closed in laughter at something Sophie, directly behind her, had said. With the sun highlighting the red highlights in her hair, and her face crinkled in laughter she was the most beautiful thing he had ever seen. She stood with her hands clasped around her huge belly, around *their* sons, protecting them even as she howled in laughter.

William tore his glance away from the love of his life and caught Art's eye, signifying with a look that their time had run out. *Drastic Measures Had To Be Taken.*

In that same instant, Petrelli—his attention obviously caught by the bell above the door ringing—stared with his mouth open in shock as Josephine entered the shop.

His reaction, startlingly quick to William who still felt drugged with the shock and fear, was to scream out the single word, "Bitch," bringing his gun around and shooting.

William would later learn that Josephine had been concentrating so heavily on what Sophie had said to make her laugh—apparently a dirty werewolf joke—that she missed the always tricky broken tile in front of the door and tripped.

From her perspective, she had merely been clumsy and tripped and fallen. From William and his brothers' heart-stopping point of view, they saw Petrelli shoot her and then Josephine fell to the ground after the loud explosion.

In that instant, a red haze of hate and angst filled William's mind and heart. His body unfroze and leapt into action. Unable to articulate his pain, William lunged for the man, knocking the offending weapon from his hand and grabbing him around the neck. Determinedly squeezing every inch of air from his lungs, William had no thought but to give some of his pain to the man who had hurt—he refused to think she was anything *except* hurt—his woman.

Tears filling his eyes, William didn't even feel the struggles of all three of his brothers trying to pry him from the suffocating man. William could hear all three of his brothers yelling at him, but in his pain, he couldn't understand a single word they uttered.

What felt like hours passed, but in reality it was barely a minute. He felt a fierce, primal satisfaction as he felt the last rasping breaths try to enter Petrelli's lungs. Still choking the man, William held not one iota of regret or sadness to be ending this man's life. Only the gaping hole where Josephine had resided could be felt, the tearing, bleeding ache in his chest, beat in time with his aching heart.

The scent of flowers surrounded him. A well-known and well-loved pair of delicate, fragile hands came to cover his own. For a split second, William could only stare incongruously at the thin feminine hands over his own on the bastard's throat.

"You know, love, I would hate to have to marry you in a jailhouse ceremony. Think of our embarrassment explaining the photos to the kids. What say you let the nasty man go?"

The thin, slightly scared voice penetrated his mind. Where he couldn't understand the words his brothers had uttered, something in his mind registered every cherished word his Josephine uttered gently to him. It was then he noticed her hands shook slightly over his own, that her face was pale and her voice was far thinner than normal.

Shock overcame his system. William instinctively let Petrelli's neck go to turn and stare at a very scared, but healthy-looking Josephine. He didn't even care that as soon as he released the jerk's throat all three of his brothers pounced on him, hogtying him with a few well-placed punches. The man didn't stand a chance in hell of getting away.

William didn't care about anything except for running his hands all over Josephine, making sure not a bruise or scratch escaped his notice.

"He shot you," he choked out, still half disbelieving the evidence his eyes were showing him. Josephine was unhurt. She wasn't bleeding, she had only grazed her palms and kneecaps falling onto the tiled café floor.

Josephine smiled down at him. She still looked too pale to his eyes, but laughter lightened her eyes, chasing away his demons.

"No, love. He shot *at* me. Klutz that I am, I tripped on the damned tile at the same time."

William didn't let her get another word out, he simply stood up and embraced her fiercely. Holding her as tightly as possible, he squeezed her huge belly against him, cradling her head as if she were a babe.

"He... You... *What* the hell are you doing down here when I told you to rest up at the house?"

William couldn't figure out exactly what he was thinking or feeling, all he knew is he wanted to feel something other than the heart-shattering intensity of believing he had lost her.

Josephine stepped back lightly, smiling gently as if she hadn't stopped him from choking a man to death seconds earlier.

"I love you too, darling. Now, I think you might have some paperwork to do, and some creative explaining to make up to explain those large dark purple bruises around the idiot's neck, hmm? Sophie and I are feeling a little tired I think and we'll just head on back to the house."

William looked to Artemais, who innocuously nudged the bound and gagged man writhing on the floor. He shrugged.

"Dom and I will go back with the girls, Samuel can go get the doc and drive him up to the house and check over Josie. You really do need to write a few reports. We can brainstorm a reason for massive fingerprints being found around his neck — right?"

William set his mouth in a hard line. He knew Art was right, but that didn't mean he had to like it. Leveling a hard glare at Josephine, he commanded in his best I-am-boss voice, "You stay in bed!"

She merely smiled at him and handed him a brown paper package. It felt like a bottle of some description.

"Sure thing, lover. Bring this home with you. Sophie introduced me to the…women's specialty store."

With sudden clarity, he knew what the bottle was, and what it contained inside of it. His anger melted into instant desire, and all he could think of was the following night.

"Sam, go get the doc. Either take him with you or get him to go and give Josephine a check-over. I have a mountain of urgent paperwork to do."

William still felt the shaking in his hands and legs, but he now had a purpose, so he pulled himself together. Write the report, lock the bastard in the single jail cell, call his deputy to watch over the moron all evening, and then get back home as quickly as possible to Josie.

Hefting the still gasping ex-cop, who stupidly was trying to mutter warnings of a lawsuit through the gag, William set to work. He had chocolate flavored paintings to draw.

Elizabeth Lapthorne

Chapter Twelve

ℬ

Josephine adjusted the enormous cotton drop cloth one last time. She was exceedingly pleased to see that her hands were steady. They no longer shook in the slightest. It had only taken a drink of hot tea, half a dozen fresh sugar cookies and twenty minutes of deep, relaxing meditation breathing exercises, as well as more than fifteen minutes of fiddling with the cloths in William's rooms, to achieve this effect.

Satisfied that not an inch of the comfortable couch showed beneath the last cloth, she stood back to admire her handiwork with a deep breath of relief. Having something to concentrate and do had done wonders for her nerves. While drinking the tea, having Sophie, Artemais, Dominic and, after the doctor had checked her over, Samuel hover over her like frantic maiden aunts did nothing but make her relive those moments of hearing the gunshot and watching William attempt murder for her.

At least she now understood the depths of his feelings for her. She doubted he lost his cool like that over someone whom he only felt an obligation toward.

She had scurried back to William's rooms pleading exhaustion as soon as she politely could. Carting all her bags and purchases with her, she had closed her mind to all the panicky thoughts and begun concentrating on setting up the rooms for her rendezvous with William later this afternoon. She had moved many of the knick-knacks and carefully pushed some of the lighter furniture out of the way, and proceeded to spread out the large, painter's cotton drop cloths she had purchased, strategically around the set of rooms. Large white cotton cloths now lay under the window, in front of the gas heater, over the mattress of William's large bed, and over his couch.

One thing she had learned from their previous experience was that chocolate body sauce was a *nightmare* to try and clean away once spilled. Many of the cushions in William's apartment had found their way to the Salvation Army, and some of the stains in the carpet would probably never come out.

So this time, forewarned by experience, Josephine had set about purchasing large cuts of the inexpensive cotton, to try and stop a repeat of her earlier mistakes. It also helped her focus on the good things in life, and not the mess from Seattle she would soon have to deal with. Everything still felt a bit shocking to her, and the last thing she wanted to do was mull over things in her head and give herself more grief and stress.

She fiddled with the satin sash of her robe, wishing the small store had more in the way of lingerie for the pregnant lady. Sophie had kindly lent her an old robe she herself had ordered specially during her pregnancy, but Josephine had resisted the impulse to order any such garments, as in a few months she would no longer require them.

Josephine crossed over to the window seat, also draped in a large cloth, to make herself comfortable and play with the paintbrush. She had no idea how long William would be. The time had alternately dragged by and simultaneously seemed to pass incredibly quickly. Josephine assured herself it was the stress and her mind decided not to linger on anything too thought provoking.

She knew tomorrow she would have to head back to Seattle, almost certainly with William, and make statements to the police, to explain her side of the story. She also knew William would want to keep tabs on the case as the evidence was collected. It was all a big mess and even thinking vaguely about it made her head pound. Obviously this was what her doctors had been meaning when they told her not to get too stressed.

Josephine rested her hands on her stomach, determined to take her mind off the darker side of her thoughts. Patting the rounded skin that she used to recognize as her stomach, she smiled as she relaxed and began to daydream about the two little boys growing inside her. Closing her eyes to picture two little Williams running around the huge old house, Josephine smiled. Maybe they'd have her characteristics, but she would be very happy with two miniature Williams running around.

Comfortable in the weak sunshine, practicing her deep meditation breathing exercises, Josephine happily daydreamed and truly relaxed for the first time since her nap.

When the door opened a short while later, she opened her eyes sleepily.

"Hey there. Paperwork all done?"

William came into the room, quietly shut the door behind him, and looked her up and down. Josephine smiled at the thought that he was checking to she if she were still in one piece.

After a moment of carefully scrutinizing her, he replied, "The paperwork is done for now. I've contacted the Seattle police, they'll be flying two detectives in tomorrow morning to go over the CDs, and take Petrelli back with them. You might need to testify, but I'll be with you every second. We can talk about this after dinner. Dominic and Samuel are lighting up the barbeque, but we have an hour or so before we need to go down."

Josephine smiled in relief. "I knew you'd be with me, but thanks for the confirmation. It's all a bit of a mess inside my head. I've been trying to work it out, but it's like trying to chase my tail, everything just spins around and around and makes me feel nauseous."

William removed his shoes and socks and walked over towards her in the window seat. Squatting, he placed his hands over her huge stomach.

"I'll definitely keep an eye on everything. Seattle was really helpful, and particularly when I explained Petrelli's involvement, they were bending over backwards to keep me in the loop. There won't be any hassles from here on in. So I want you to concentrate on getting much bigger and enjoying our babies."

Josephine smiled and began to unbutton his shirt. "What was that you mentioned about having an hour until the barbeque will be ready?"

William smiled and began to unbutton his pants. Just as he shucked them over his hips, he raised an eyebrow as Josephine stopped taking his shirt off. "Aren't you going to finish this?" he teased.

Josephine didn't reply, but reached behind her underneath the pillows on the window seat.

Brandishing her paintbrush, she hefted herself out of the window seat and crossed over to the table where she had laid his bottle of chocolate sauce.

"I decided to do something with all that nervous energy, and look what I miraculously seem to find! A bottle of chocolate body paint complete with a paintbrush. How convenient," she teased over her shoulder as she rummaged for the extra paintbrush hidden behind the cushion.

Before she could turn around with the bottle in her hand, William had crept up behind her. She discovered he had stripped his shirt off when he grabbed her in a big bear embrace from behind. The warmth of his chest was a welcome sensation. She giggled as he slowly walked them both plastered together, towards the bed.

"I'm sure there's a good reason why there are huge cotton sheets draped everywhere around here?"

Josephine laughed with delight. "Do you really want to replace another set of sheets and covers?"

"Ahhh," he grumbled, low in his throat, "that's definitely smart thinking on your part."

Quickly glancing around, he chuckled. "The window seat? In front of the heater?" Craning his head, he laughed at the numerous sheets she had laid out. "The *mini* bar?"

Josephine laughed. "Well, I thought we might get thirsty with all this chocolate, and then not feel like moving, and the mini bar is where all the water is…"

William gave Josephine a slight shove, so she fell down onto the bed. "Let's start at the beginning, hmm? Work our way around the room and see how long the sauce lasts."

Snatching the brush from her hand, he opened the bottle and dipped the brush in. Josephine opened and removed her robe, eyeing William's naked chest.

"I think I should get to start with the brush — I've had the biggest shocks this afternoon," she said with a grin.

William looked seriously at her for a moment, the concern and fear still reflected in his deep blue eyes. For just a second, the tidal wave of emotion swept over them both, threatening to drown her in its depth. With a small smile, William brandished the brush in the air.

"Not a chance, darling. The scares and emotion you felt were nothing to the devastation I felt when I thought that jerk had shot you. Anyway, I have the brush, therefore I get to draw first. Be a good girl and wait your turn. It will take a few years at the least for me to recuperate the years I lost in the stress of this afternoon."

Josephine sighed, surreptitiously moving her hand under the sheet and pillow. Grabbing the other paintbrush she had bought, knowing she would need it, she pulled it out.

"Fine. Be mean. Now give me some of that sauce, buddy."

William drew slow, lazy circles around her full breasts, patterns down her stomach, all the while trying to keep the sauce out of Josephine's reach.

The full bottle sloshed a little onto the cotton, but neither of them paid much attention, both of them too focused on their mini war. Josephine snuck a few decent swirls onto William's chest herself, but ten minutes later, William set aside his brush, declaring the end to their match. Naturally, she was covered head to foot in the sauce, and he only had a few dabs on his chest and back. Panting slightly from her exertions, she lay back on the bed, snuggling into the warmth of the pillows and incredibly grateful she had replaced the usual sheets with the white cotton cloths.

"This is insanely unfair," she complained. "My Sauce, My Rules. Now hand it over."

William merely grinned as Josephine held out one arm, barely able to conceal her panting from their play. When William smiled down at her he showed all of his teeth, reminding her of the wolf he became.

"My Bed, My Rules."

Josephine crossed her arms over her chest, smearing chocolate sauce everywhere.

"Well, mister, I seem to be lying in this bed, too—so it's *our* bed."

Super-quickly, William dropped the bottle on the bedside table and snatched her brush from her hand and laid it aside. Moving back to pin Josephine down with his part of his body, he pressed her into the soft cotton and covers.

"I want to taste my masterpiece."

With that, he bent down and slowly ran his tongue around the outermost circle on her breast. The sensation of his wet, warm tongue, roughly lapping over her skin, silenced Josephine. Too busy with their play arguing, she had completely forgotten to prepare herself for the sensation of William licking her skin clean.

"Uhhh…" she managed to groan as she grabbed his shoulders to draw him closer.

The wet heat of his mouth penetrated her skin and set her nerves tingling. Rational thought flew from her mind and white noise filled her head, the roar echoing in her ears.

Slowly, William lapped up every speck of the chocolate sauce circle. When he paused, she cracked an eye open, trying to coordinate the words to inquire why he had stopped.

When he saw he had her attention, he smiled softly down at her. "One," he counted, then bent back down to start laving the next circle closer in to her nipple.

Throwing her head back in defeat, Josephine quickly counted. There were another four circles until he would reach her nipple, and there were three circles on her other breast. There were a number of squiggles on her stomach, and a few on her face. If William took this long on all of her circles, she would be a mindless mess before he even came close to finishing her off!

Determined, Josephine rallied her strength and levered herself up off the soft bed. Surprising William with her move, he tilted himself onto his side, not willing to accidentally squash her or the babies.

Josephine reversed their positions, tumbling William down onto his back as she straddled his thighs. The back part of her brain knew he *let* her shove him around, but because she won, she wasn't going to complain.

Josephine took both of his hands, and raised them above his head. Half holding them both in one of her small hands, showing him what she wanted him to do, she silently thanked him as he held still. Her smaller hands barely gripped his two much bigger ones, but the glint in his eye told her he would play along—for now.

She reached over to nab the bottle of paint. As she settled herself fully on him once more, he raised an eyebrow mockingly at her.

"You move too slow," she complained, upending the bottle of sauce onto his chest. A huge glob of the sauce fell out of the bottle. Shakily, Josephine returned the bottle to the bedside table.

Letting go of William's hands, shining a brilliant smile on him when he didn't move them from above his head, Josephine started spreading the rich sauce over his chest and abdomen. Playing as if it were finger-paint, she created swirls and patterns in the mess.

Moving down so her belly lay cradled between William's spread thighs, Josephine could easily lap at the sauce, now much thinner as it was spread liberally around William's large chest.

"You move too fast," William complained, an imitation of her earlier complaint about him.

"Really?"

Palming his sacs, gently stroking the soft skin, Josephine played with the lightly patched hair on his chest. Tugging with teeth and tongue, Josephine nibbled her way around his chest, smearing more sauce everywhere and messing up her face.

Giving her a few more minutes to relish the control she had won, William gently moved his arms so he could idly stroke her back and shoulders, enjoying her silky skin. Josephine murmured her approval.

As she moved her way lower and lower, just as she decided to take the head of his cock in her mouth and *really* get the action moving, William gently flipped them both over again, so she lay on her side, and he rested at her back, a bare whisper along her skin. He didn't press his weight down on her, so she wasn't forced onto her stomach, not wanting to hurt the babies in any way, but by the mere sensation of him along her back her breathing speeded up.

"Now who's moving too slow?" he taunted her.

Josephine looked at the chocolate-smeared drop sheet, and smiled. "You're ruining the sheets, chocolate stains remember?"

"We'll buy some more for next time," he replied, nipping at her neck, totally unconcerned.

Josephine giggled, a feminine, unconcerned sound. "Better buy stock in cotton then."

William gently bit her neck, sucking on the spot where he had already branded her, unconsciously re-marking her as his. They both knew the truth, but something inside him needed to taste his mark again, to warn others away. As he laved the spot, Josephine wiggled her ass deeper into the cradle of his hips.

"Come on," she complained, "you started this, you can bite me later."

Laughing aloud at the impatience in her voice, William refrained from pointing out it was *she* who bought the sauce and started this. He wasn't going to ruin this moment.

He nibbled a path directly down her spine, laving the dimples down at her ass. When he spread her legs to give himself access to her creaming pussy, he enjoyed the choking breaths coming from his love.

Eagerly, he lapped at her juices, drawing out the moment as long as she could bear. When she started whimpering, begging him to enter her, he merely rumbled against her clit, the vibrations from his throat pushing her higher.

When Josephine started screaming in earnest, as her first peak hit her, he dragged himself back up to stretch along her body, not wanting to excite her overly much in case it induced a premature labor.

"Are you ready?" he breathed into her ear.

"Right now," she gasped, trying to catch her breath.

Gently but firmly, he stroked into her, long and deep. As he felt her tight inner walls caress his cock, he groaned and rested his head in the curve of her shoulder. Pausing fully inside her to relish the moment, he took a deep breath and slowly, carefully withdrew.

The friction caused them both to groan, the pleasure intense. Slowly moving inside her, pushing them both up their peak, William couldn't help himself from moving faster and faster. Gently caressing her clit, he made sure his Josephine was with him every step of the way, thrusting back onto him, rubbing herself against him, pulling her thighs up closer to him and wrapping his arms tighter around her.

When they both exploded, their cries mingled as his seed drenched her. Spooning their bodies together, not wanting to rest his weight down on her stomach even for a moment, William nuzzled her.

"What did you do?" Josephine finally managed to ask, when her heartbeat had settled down somewhat.

William chuckled, "I think they call it making love, but we can look it up later."

"No, I meant when you bit my neck. I can feel that you didn't break the skin, but it tingles, it feels…different."

William thought carefully about his words. "You know that I have already marked you, so everyone else would realize you're mine. I just, I don't know, wanted to reassure myself it was still there. It's simply claiming you as mine, a declaration like marriage vows."

Josephine thought for a few minutes, pondering over his words and their meaning. William waited, silently, knowing there would be more questions.

"Will you need to mark our sons?"

"No, love. They'll scent of you and me. It will be obvious to all whom they belong to."

Josephine nodded and snuggled into his warmth. "Can we nap before dinner?"

He laughed. "How about a long shower and then maybe a nap? We don't want to stain the sheets, and I don't want you to nap without blankets covering you. I know I can keep you warm, but the breeze around here can often get chilly."

Josephine squeezed her eyes shut. "I can't get up, not even for a shower. See, my eyes are shut."

"Ah well, a bath it is then. I guess I'll just have to carry you."

Slowly, she moved out of bed. "No! It's okay, I don't need you breaking your back, thanks all the same."

William looked her in the eye, very serious again. "I can easily lift you, Josephine, don't worry about me. But now that you're up, let's go get cleaned up."

Rolling her eyes at his tricky mind, Josephine smiled and *slowly* raced him to the bathroom. "Last one in has to clean up the sheets!"

Epilogue

℘

"Do you accept the serious and permanent position of Godparents to this young man, eldest child of William and Josephine Rutledge?"

"We do," Artemais and Sophie responded, holding out Alexander Thomas to the priest. The elderly man took the offered child, cradling him into one arm while the other hand dipped into the fount of holy water.

"I now christen you Alexander Thomas Rutledge," the priest intoned, sprinkling holy water on the four-months-old baby's head.

At the chilly water touching his brow, Alexander Thomas scrunched up his face and pouted for a moment. Flailing his arms about, fully expecting any one of a half-dozen well-known and loved adults to pick up and hold his hand, to soothe him. When only the priest's blessings continued to fall down upon the young man, he opened one beautiful blue eye.

Only seeing a strange face holding him, he emitted a loud, lusty cry expressing his distaste for such matters.

When the priest simply poured more holy water on his head, hurrying through the blessings of the dedication ritual, young Alexander Thomas screamed louder.

Sophie looked back to the front pew, where Christiana sat in her baby basket, happily playing with her toys, completely oblivious to her young cousin's disgust.

As the priest continued to sprinkle the holy water onto the child, his wails became louder.

"Oh, for heaven's sake," Josephine muttered. Carefully placing a pristine and thankfully sleeping Samantha Monique into Samuel's waiting arms, she crossed over to the priest to take her screaming son from him. She turned him so his head was still in reach of the priest, but cradled his body against her familiar warmth to soothe him and hopefully halt his cries.

The priest, not liking to rush through the ritual, gladly let the mother take her screaming baby.

Samantha Monique woke up at the change of hands, opened her identical blue eyes and saw one of her favorite uncles holding her. She snuggled into his arms, only slightly ruffling her dainty white dress, when she heard the unmistakable wail of her twin brother.

With an uncanny knowledge only her parents seemed to understand, Samantha Monique knew her brother was crying because he was upset at something. Not knowing or caring why her older brother was creating such a fuss, she opened her mouth and added her screams to his. Samuel tried to bounce her, calm her, but nothing he cooed to her helped soothe her.

"You're losing your touch, brother dear—next thing you know you'll be asking my help to pick up the ladies." Dominic grinned at his brother. "Hand her over to me, I have never yet met a lady I couldn't charm like a bird."

Knowing that Samantha Monique wouldn't settle down until she knew her twin was soothed and happy, Samuel shrugged and handed his soon-to-be Goddaughter over.

Dominic made his silly baby face and started chatting to her about computer code—actions that almost always won his little soon-to-be Goddaughter over. Today, it made her pause and wait. Swiveling her head as much as possible, she obviously sought for her twin, whose wails were subsiding, but who still whimpered in disgust.

Dominic caught Josephine's eye. She was standing by the fount of holy water, squashed between Art and Sophie, holding her son. She gestured with her head to bring Samantha Monique over to them.

Both Samuel and Dominic crossed over to the fount quickly, passing Artemais and Sophie as they returned to their seat beside Christiana. Samuel cringed when he realized that Samantha Monique was almost certain to scream at the cold holy water as Alexander had.

Samantha and Alexander looked at one another as the priest reached out to hold Samantha.

"Do you accept the serious and permanent position of Godparents to this young lady, eldest daughter of William and Josephine Rutledge?" the priest repeated to Samuel and Dominic.

"We do," they responded.

"I now christen you Samantha Monique Rutledge," the priest repeated, sprinkling holy water onto her forehead.

Obviously not expecting such horrid treatment from a man—every man she knew spoiled her rotten and obeyed her every wish—Samantha started shrieking, expressing her disapproval.

Alexander Thomas started squirming in his mother's arms, expressing his joint disapproval.

The priest whipped through his blessings and sprinkled a little more holy water on both their foreheads, for luck. Moving the entire Rutledge party on, they soon stood outside in the sunshine.

Josephine and Sophie laughed. "You'd think they had something against screaming children! I'm sure every baby I've ever seen dedicated or blessed has screamed in objection to having cold holy water shoved in their face!"

Josephine laughed as William caught up with the ladies and threw his arms around his wife.

"I swear it must be your genes that caused the kids to do that. I don't think we Rutledge men ever screamed when we had holy water splashed all over us."

Josephine laughed and leaned into his embrace. "I will remind you it was *your* son who started this. Samantha was sleeping peacefully before Alexander woke her up."

William merely rolled his eyes. "Honestly, you women! You're all just trying to gang up on us poor men. I shall have to have words with the person who told you there were *two* boys inside you. I think little Samantha might object."

Josephine laughed and kissed her husband, letting them lag behind the rest of the group.

"Don't worry…we can have another boy next time."

"Mmm…I like the sound of that. We really should practice a little more, you know?"

"Well, Sophie and I went shopping this morning…" she trailed off as William's breath caught and increased.

"Don't! Save it 'til we get home or I'll rush you right now."

Josephine smiled her secret little smile.

Life was good.

Also by Elizabeth Lapthorne

❧

Behind the Mask (*anthology*)
Bonded for Eternity
Ellora's Cavemen: Legendary Tails I (*anthology*)
Kinkily Ever After
Lion In Love
Merc and Her Men
Montague Vampires 1: Heated Fantasies
Montague Vampires 2: Flaming Fantasies
Montague Vampires 3: Secret Fantasies
Montague Vampires: Desperate and Dateless
Payback
Rutledge Werewolves 1: Scent of Passion
Rutledge Werewolves 3: The Mating Game
Rutledge Werewolves 4: My Heart's Passion
Rutledge Werewolves 5: Chasing Love

About the Author

Elizabeth Lapthorne has been writing professionally since 2002. She has been astonished by the sucess of her Rutledge Werewolf series, and finds immense pleasure in hearing from her fans. To date she has more than ten books out, a few of those even in paperback.

Elizabeth regularly goes to the gym to chew over her ideas; many a book has begun or been worked through while cycling on the bikes. She also loves to read, eat chocolate and talk for hours with her friends. Elizabeth would love to hear from her fans, and checks her email religiously.

Elizabeth welcomes comments from readers. You can find her website and email address on her author bio page at www.ellorascave.com.

Tell Us What You Think

We appreciate hearing reader opinions about our books. You can email us at Comments@EllorasCave.com.

Why an electronic book?

We live in the Information Age — an exciting time in the history of human civilization, in which technology rules supreme and continues to progress in leaps and bounds every minute of every day. For a multitude of reasons, more and more avid literary fans are opting to purchase e-books instead of paper books. The question from those not yet initiated into the world of electronic reading is simply: *Why?*

1. ***Price.*** An electronic title at Ellora's Cave Publishing and Cerridwen Press runs anywhere from 40% to 75% less than the cover price of the exact same title in paperback format. Why? Basic mathematics and cost. It is less expensive to publish an e-book (no paper and printing, no warehousing and shipping) than it is to publish a paperback, so the savings are passed along to the consumer.

2. ***Space.*** Running out of room in your house for your books? That is one worry you will never have with electronic books. For a low one-time cost, you can purchase a handheld device specifically designed for e-reading. Many e-readers have large, convenient screens for viewing. Better yet, hundreds of titles can be stored within your new library — on a single microchip. There are a variety of e-readers from different manufacturers. You can also read e-books on your PC or laptop computer. (Please note that Ellora's Cave does not endorse any specific brands.

You can check our websites at www.ellorascave.com or www.cerridwenpress.com for information we make available to new consumers.)

3. *Mobility.* Because your new e-library consists of only a microchip within a small, easily transportable e-reader, your entire cache of books can be taken with you wherever you go.

4. *Personal Viewing Preferences.* Are the words you are currently reading too small? Too large? Too… ANNOYING? Paperback books cannot be modified according to personal preferences, but e-books can.

5. *Instant Gratification.* Is it the middle of the night and all the bookstores near you are closed? Are you tired of waiting days, sometimes weeks, for bookstores to ship the novels you bought? Ellora's Cave Publishing sells instantaneous downloads twenty-four hours a day, seven days a week, every day of the year. Our webstore is never closed. Our e-book delivery system is 100% automated, meaning your order is filled as soon as you pay for it.

Those are a few of the top reasons why electronic books are replacing paperbacks for many avid readers.

As always, Ellora's Cave and Cerridwen Press welcome your questions and comments. We invite you to email us at Comments@ellorascave.com or write to us directly at Ellora's Cave Publishing Inc., 1056 Home Avenue, Akron, OH 44310-3502.

erridwen, the Celtic Goddess of wisdom, was the muse who brought inspiration to storytellers and those in the creative arts. Cerridwen Press encompasses the best and most innovative stories in all genres of today's fiction. Visit our site and discover the newest titles by talented authors who still get inspired - much like the ancient storytellers did, once upon a time.

Cerridwen Press

www.cerridwenpress.com